stealing the bachelor

a Stealing the Heart novel

SONYA WEISS

This book is a work of fiction. Names, characters, places, and incidents are the product of the author's imagination or are used fictitiously. Any resemblance to actual events, locales, or persons, living or dead, is coincidental.

Entangled Publishing, LLC
2614 South Timberline Road
Suite 109
Fort Collins, CO 80525
Visit our website at www.entangledpublishing.com.

Bliss is an imprint of Entangled Publishing, LLC. For more information on our titles, visit http://www.entangledpublishing.com/category/bliss

Edited by Alycia Tornetta
Cover design by Heather Howland
Cover art from iStock

Manufactured in the United States of America

First Edition January 2016

Bliss

For the minions, always, and Alycia Tornetta, an editor with a magic wand.

Chapter One

Mug shot. Orange jumpsuit. Details on the evening news.

I could go to prison. Ann Snyder took a deep breath to calm herself. She tried again to get the handcuffs clamped around her wrists off. They were part of a Halloween costume she planned to wear, and she'd put them on to see how she'd look when she was hauled off and locked away. Only now she couldn't find the key. But that was the least of her worries right now.

She'd practically worn a hole in the hardwood flooring with all the pacing back and forth. She pivoted, then stopped abruptly. It was time to act. Knowing who she had to turn to didn't make it any easier to swallow. She pressed a hand against her stomach, the handcuffs jiggling while her trepidation grew to the size of a small truck.

Usually, she was the calm one—if she didn't count dumping a bowl of melted chocolate over Monica Sinclair's head. But the woman had slept with Ann's fiancé and then gloated about it all over town. She'd waltzed into the chocolate shop recently and made snide comments about Ann having put on a few pounds. Monica had had the chocolate coming. Even after losing her fiancé to a woman like that, Ann had tried to find the bright side, to look for the positives, the rainbow after the storm.

But there was absolutely nothing positive about what was happening now. She'd been stabbed in the back. Now, because of her misplaced trust, the business she loved could go belly up. For the love of her business—and for that reason only—she was ready to face attorney Eric Maxwell, the man she'd done her best to avoid since high school. She needed him to keep her next fashion accessory from being an orange prison jumpsuit, and she needed him to save her business. She had no choice except to throw herself on his mercy. Under the pinch financially and too proud to ask her family for a dime, she'd have to see if she couldn't get him to skip the retainer and take small payments. Maybe he'd be willing to do that.

She changed—with much difficulty—out of her paint-stained jeans with the holes in the knees into a simple black skirt, pairing it with low-heeled shoes. Her shirt would have to do. She couldn't change it thanks to the handcuffs. For good luck, she added one of her mother's antique necklaces. Leaving her shoulder length brown hair down, she added a touch of lipstick, and headed out.

The trip through the heart of Sweet Creek never failed to make Ann appreciate the sight. She'd been born and raised in the small town. She loved the simplicity of the place, the feeling of neighborliness, and the beauty of the quaint buildings. Singing along with the James Morrison song on the radio, she tried to keep the worst of her fear at bay. By the time she parked her little pale blue Volkswagen in the lot behind the building that housed the law firm where Eric worked, the sky had opened up and unleashed a steady shower of rain. Rain in October and the chill in the air always made her feel the pang from missing her late parents. Had they been alive, they would no doubt have been disappointed in her latest failure. *No*, Ann shook her head. Her business wouldn't fail. She'd poured her heart into it and every bit of her savings. Failure couldn't happen.

Squaring her shoulders and swallowing her pride, she stepped out into the rain, then dashed for the protection of the awning. She jerked open the office door, rushed into the foyer, and promptly slipped on the slick floor.

To keep from face planting, she slammed her hands against the wall, wincing when the force stung her fingers.

"Are you okay?"

Through the strands of her dripping hair, she locked gazes with Eric Maxwell. The floor she was standing on free-fell a hundred stories. His dark chestnut hair glistened under the lighting. Instead of his usual suit and quirky nerd ties, he wore a pair of jeans and a T-shirt, which were as soaked as her own clothes. The T-shirt clung to his wet skin, providing a great outline of his nicely muscled abs.

When did he get those, and where has he been hiding them? He hadn't had them in high school.

Remembering him as a teenager brought back the sting of how he'd humiliated her. His friends had created a fantasy girl draft and listed all the girls in their school and their physical attributes in great detail. When one of them had mentioned her name, Eric had quickly and loudly said, "Ann Snyder doesn't belong on that list. She's not in the same class as those girls." His voice had carried down the hallway to her, and she'd been on the receiving end of laughter and pitying glances.

She'd ducked into the girls' bathroom and cried. She knew she wasn't the beauty her sisters were, but to hear it confirmed had hurt. As the years had passed, she'd chalked it up to high school drama and thought maybe Eric hadn't meant what he'd said. Especially after he'd blatantly hinted that he liked her. She'd even considered going out with him.

But then she'd overheard him, again, at her sister Abby's diner with his old high school friends. Loudmouth Jerry had laughingly asked, "Did Ann Snyder ever make your fantasy list?" and Eric had looked disgusted and said that she'd never be on such a list.

After that, she'd cold-shouldered Eric, never wanting to feel that way again.

"Ann?"

She blinked and pushed the hurt aside. This wasn't high school anymore, and it didn't matter that she wasn't as pretty as her sisters or any of the girls on his fantasy list. She had a good life and her business. If she could keep it. She took a deep breath. "First, get me out of these handcuffs."

His mouth dropped open, then he snapped it closed. He stared at her for a second before he said, "I don't even want to know. Your private life is your business."

Swallowing the embarrassment of what he must be thinking, Ann said, "Can you help me or not? It's not what you think." Her gaze drifted across his muscles before she snapped her attention back to his eyes. "Keep me out of handcuffs. Legally. Not that I would need you illegally." She pressed a hand against the side of her head for a second, then rattled the handcuffs. "Well?"

He stepped closer and raised her arms. Lowering his head, he leaned in to examine the handcuffs. "Where's the key?"

"If I knew that, I wouldn't be wearing them."

He patted the pockets of his jeans. "I don't have anything that could cut them."

"Would you normally?"

"I like to be prepared."

"For *handcuffs*?"

"Hold on." He gripped the chain between the cuffs and pulled. It snapped like it was nothing more than paper.

Ann licked her lips. "Um…thanks." She rubbed her wrists. After she left here, she'd figure out how to get the bracelet part of the cuffs off. Surely her thoughts were a bit fuzzy because she'd skipped breakfast this morning. But those muscles… She snuck another glance before blurting out, "You're wet."

He gave a look that said that was obvious. "I got drenched on the way in." He crossed his arms, jerking his head toward the entrance. "You're the last person I expected to come through those doors." His tone wasn't exactly unwelcoming, but it wasn't welcoming, either. She couldn't read what was going on behind that mask of his.

"I never thought I'd ever have a reason to come to your office." Ann glanced around at the empty area surrounding them before looking back up at him. His gaze held hers. Uncomfortable with the prolonged silence and the butterflies in her stomach, she asked, "Where's your secretary?"

"I gave her the day off. I have some business to take care of with my family." His lips tightened when he mentioned family, and he shook his head. "It doesn't matter. What do you need?" he said, his deep voice slightly exasperated.

"I told you already. You." Keeping her focus on his handsome face, she said, "I need you. Desperately."

He raised his eyebrows and crossed his arms, staring at her without saying a word. *How can he say so much without speaking?* She hated feeling like she'd rolled into town and fell off the turnip truck. Embarrassed and irritated with herself, Ann clarified, "I mean, I need your services. Your skills as an attorney. Nothing else." She blinked away droplets of water that dripped from her hair onto her eyelashes.

He gave her a long, steady look from his dark chocolate eyes, and Ann's stomach tightened. She hated that. Hated that she couldn't quite figure out what was going on. There was that tension she noticed every time she was around him, making her feel awkward and definitely not calm or quick-witted.

Finally, after lasering her with his eyes, Eric motioned her forward. "Come with me." He led the way to his spacious, richly furnished office and disappeared into a small adjoining bathroom, then returned with two oversize towels. "This should help absorb some of the water."

Ann took the towel he offered and began drying the ends of her hair, then rubbed it along her arms, darting a glance at him as he slipped off his T-shirt, giving her a front row seat to his impressive physique. She gaped as he dried himself and then put on a clean shirt.

When he saw her watching, he said, "It's the only T-shirt I have at the office. I would have offered it to you, but I didn't think you'd want it."

Checking out the *Star Wars* logo on the shirt, Ann said, "I love *Star Wars*." *What's going on? I sound like Nerd Girl, and Eric looks too hot for words. Maybe I hit my head when I slipped.*

"You want me to take it off? That way you can wear it and get out of your wet clothes?" He walked around the expansive desk.

She lifted her gaze to his. *Is he teasing*? No, he couldn't be. His expression was serious and besides, Eric never playfully teased her. Still, there was something about his voice that suddenly sent shivers chasing up her spine. *Get a grip, girl.* "Thanks for the offer, but if I take you up on it, then all I'd have on is a T-shirt." *Duh.* She gave herself a mental forehead slap.

His gaze dropped to her legs.

Her insides heated up hot enough to deep fry something. All the air in the room snapped with increased tension. "You taking off the T-shirt would be a bad idea. Gorgeous men without their shirts on are always…" Her voice trailed off, and she gritted her teeth. *Why am I babbling?*

"Gorgeous men?" He frowned, and his gaze sharpened into something she couldn't define. "Are you saying you think I'm gorgeous?"

"No, of course not. I've never noticed your looks." *And Ann's nose grew two sizes that day…* Ann squelched the taunting thought. She'd seen Eric hundreds of times but never really paid attention until…now. Was she *ever* paying attention now. And it was unfair that he was so polished and smooth, so *him*, and she still felt as gangly and awkward as she always had.

He inclined his head slightly, waiting for her to speak.

Uncomfortable with how he was watching her, and telling herself to stay focused, she searched through her purse, removing the papers she'd been given. "I think I'm in trouble." She unfolded them and passed the stack to him, hating how her hand shook slightly. "When I arrived at my business this morning, it was crawling with various alphabet agencies. The expressions on the faces of everyone there scared me. I asked one of the agents from the FDA what was going on, and she gave me those documents." Ann shuddered at the memory of the exact moment she'd realized everything was about to hit the fan.

His gaze sharpened. "Your business was raided? What would they want with Chocolate Cravings?"

"I know, right? I was about to make a joke about them jonesing for chocolate, but then one of them handed me a search warrant. I think I'm in trouble."

He skimmed the papers, his expression darkening. Then he looked at her, his expression incredulous. "If any of these accusations are even remotely true, you're right about being in trouble." Tapping his index finger on the first sheet of paper, he said, "This says that you engaged in deceptive trade practices, among other things."

"Deceptive trade practices?"

"Your company sold goods labeled as one thing when they were actually another."

Ann put the towel down on the leather chair across from the desk and took a seat, hoping to keep the wet material of her skirt from dripping onto the expensive furniture. "I would never do something like that. All the labels on my chocolates are correct, and the ingredients are clearly listed."

He shook his head and explained, "They're not talking about the chocolates. What they're saying is that you sold health supplements under your company's name claiming they cured illnesses."

"But I didn't sell any supplements." Her heart beat faster. She didn't like the sound of this.

He shrugged. "According to these papers, you did. With the FDA and the IRS both involved, this is the big league. It's federal level, meaning federal courts. There's a copy of a cease and desist letter that was sent to your company four weeks ago. You were warned to stop selling the supplements."

Her fear rose along with her voice. "Today is the first time I've seen it. Lewis always picks up the mail." Because she'd trusted her manager. *That rat.* She'd never even laid eyes on the cease and desist letter. *Wait a second.* Hope rose within her. She couldn't be responsible for something she didn't know anything about, and she'd tell the FDA exactly that. Maybe then they'd realize that this was all a huge mistake. She told Eric as much, then smoothed her skirt and smiled. "Who knows? Maybe I won't even need an attorney."

Eric leaned back in his chair and narrowed his eyes. She'd never noticed before today how tall he was and how well he filled out his clothes. His slight smile made her restless. "Your business became financially successful pretty fast. Quicker than normal, wouldn't you agree?"

"Well...yes," Ann said, not understanding. So what if her business had taken off? She'd put in plenty of long hours and hard work to make it happen, even peeling off the layers of old wallpaper herself. Many evenings she'd worked past midnight, scraping the walls until her fingertips cracked because she couldn't afford to hire help.

"With the amount of money you made, there's no way you were only selling chocolates. The supplements were shipped in bags with your company logo. You don't know *anything* about those?" Eric steepled his fingers, one eyebrow raised.

Her temper rising at his skeptical tone, Ann glared. "It was *only* chocolates, and no, I didn't know about the bags."

"But you knew about the supplements?"

"No."

"Weren't you the one who ordered the bags? Didn't you notice how many bags you were going through versus how many 'supposed chocolates' you were actually selling? You recently took a trip to Hawaii. How'd you afford that? Did you jet off to relax while preying on the hopes of other people?"

Ann blinked, taken aback by his rapid-fire questions and his air quotes around the words supposed chocolates. "Yes, about the bags—"

"So you admit you knew the bags were used for the supplements?"

"What?" Ann stammered out. "No! And 'supposed chocolates?' Preying on the hopes…" Ann shifted her feet, preparing to stand. She couldn't wait to get out of his office. Granted, she and Eric weren't friends, but she'd never expected him to be so hateful, like he was enjoying her misery. Before she could stand, he fired another round of questions at her.

"You and your manager Lewis are involved romantically, correct? You'd do anything for him. Was the plan to scam people solely your idea or was it a joint effort?"

"Lewis and I were friends, nothing more, and I haven't scammed anyone." She'd thought that Lewis was different.

That he was trustworthy. He'd been so kind, always thoughtful. Ann cringed inwardly. Of course he had. He'd only acted like a great guy so he could use her business. She'd been an easy mark. Why did she always have such bad luck with men? Did she have a giant bull's-eye on her back?

"I think that you knew what Lewis was doing but decided to turn a blind eye toward it."

"I didn't know." Ann had to fight to keep from crying. "I'm leaving. Coming here was a mistake. How can you speak to me like this?"

His voice gentled. "I don't for one second believe you're guilty of anything, Ann. I talked to you that way because that's exactly how a prosecutor will come at you. Nothing will be off limits. Your character, your relationships, everything about you will be called into question. Just because you're innocent doesn't mean anything. Do you see how easy it is to fluster someone?"

"You said those things just to prove a point?" Ann slumped in the chair, suddenly drained.

"I did. If you were honest with yourself, you'd admit that you need me and," his voice deepened, quiet and sexy, "you want me."

Chapter Two

"*Want you?*"

"Yes, and you know it."

He didn't imagine the flash of anger on her face. He'd meant want as in *want* him as an attorney. Waiting for the impossible was something he knew better than to do. He was the nerd, and girls like her didn't choose nerds. How many times had he wished he could come up with a way for her to overlook his geek status and really see him for who he was? But he'd chickened out. Too afraid to try.

Now, he sensed that maybe, just maybe, he was about to be handed a chance. If he helped her with her case, they'd have to spend time together, which meant he could prove to her that he was more than just a nerd. Maybe he could end up with the one woman his heart had always wanted.

Seconds ticked by. His best guess was that she was warring between anger at him and her pride, but what good was pride when she was facing this mess? He tried again. "You want my expertise, which means that you need me, correct?"

Her gaze raked him, and she didn't answer for several

minutes. Finally, she said, "You're right. I do need you. Will you take the case?"

"I will." He grabbed a pen and reached for a yellow legal pad on his desk. Thank God he could keep his hands busy to take his mind off how great she looked. Ann had the kind of girl-next-door beauty that often made him lose his train of thought around her. He cleared his throat to get back on track. "Let's go over a few things. You said Lewis picks up the mail. When was the last time that you spoke to him?" He'd never liked the man, but this was different from him not liking the majority of the men who'd been in Ann's life. She'd always chosen bad boys, and since Eric had been the nerd in high school, she'd never had any interest in him.

"I saw him yesterday before he left for Indiana to visit his sick grandmother."

Eric couldn't help himself. His lips twisted in disbelief. "Sick grandmother? I highly doubt that. I still can't believe you hired Lewis after I warned you about him."

"Thanks for the I-told-you-so." Ann rubbed her temple. "I know that you don't care for Lewis, but—wait a second..." She squeezed her hands together. "Earlier you said I was being charged with mislabeling a product among other things. What other things? What else do they think I did?"

"The reason I don't like Lewis is because he's always been a jerk who can't be trusted, and he's proved that by running away, leaving you to face the consequences." Eric wasn't glad for her heartache, but he was thankful the other man was gone. "As far as the other things I mentioned, you're being accused of scheming to get people to invest in the supplement business and then stealing their money. I wouldn't be surprised if other government agencies come looking for you."

"Other agencies? Stealing money?" Her voice squeaked, and Ann swallowed before she continued. "I've never stolen anything in my life. Well, except a palm-size bouncy ball, but I was four years old, and my mom caught me, made me take it back, and apologize. Then she grounded me for a week." She closed her eyes for a second, winced, then opened them and said, "I hate the idea that anyone was taken advantage of. I'll pay it all back. How much money are we talking about?"

Eric scanned the paperwork and then whistled before looking at her. "A little over a quarter of a million dollars."

Ann gasped, putting a hand up to her chest. "I don't have that kind of money." She took another deep breath. "Please tell me that's everything."

"The IRS has taken the money that was in your business bank account." He felt bad and wished he wasn't the bearer of the bad news when he saw her shocked expression.

"Can they do that without letting me know first? Without a court order?" She rolled the strap of her purse over and over in her hand, then stopped. "This can't be right."

"An investigation was opened through their Criminal Investigation Division, because money was acquired by your business through illegal means. They don't need a court order."

"But…I haven't transferred money from my business account to my personal one yet this month. I don't have any money now. Not that there was much to begin with, because I paid off some bills and put the rest of last month's profit back into the business. So, I'm broke." She blew out her breath as realization set in. "I'd thought maybe I could talk to you about taking payments to help me. Without my money, I can't afford to pay you or any other attorney to help." She rose and paced the room. "This is something that Lewis will straighten out. I know he will. I'll call him."

Eric's gaze never left her face. He'd dealt with one too many con men in the course of his career, and everything he knew about Lewis fit that description. "My guess is that he's already on his way to a country that doesn't have an extradition treaty with the United States."

Ann's steps faltered. "He wouldn't."

"You want to bet?" Eric folded his arms, hating that a man so unworthy of Ann had won her trust. "Go ahead and call him."

Her face flushed. "You don't have to look so smug about this."

"I wasn't aware that I was. Do you think I'm enjoying your predicament?" He wasn't. He hated that her life was in turmoil.

"I don't know. Are you?"

"You're upset, and that's understandable, but I'm not the villain here."

"You're right. I'm sorry." With hands that shook, Ann took out her cell phone, turned on the speaker, and hit the speed dial, sending Eric a pained smile. *The number you have dialed is no longer in service.* She ended the call. "I kept a small splinter of hope alive that Lewis wasn't behind this, but I guess it's true." Dropping the phone back into her purse, she looked across at Eric. "Since I can't afford a lawyer, I guess I should start researching how to make prison orange look good with my skin tone."

Thinking fast, he saw his chance to help her—and maybe win her heart. He decided to take it. "We can work out my fees by bartering."

She looked cautiously optimistic and motioned with her fingers. "Give it to me straight. What do you want?"

"I need you to date me."

Her beautiful eyes widened and then her lips tightened with anger. Putting her hands on her hips, she said, "Is Monica not enough for you? What makes you think that I'd help you cheat? Is this supposed to be some kind of twisted joke? She cheats with my boyfriend, and I'm supposed to cheat with hers?"

He could never seem to find the right words to say around Ann. Pretty sad for a guy who made his living arguing with his words. She had the power to make him feel like a hopeful schoolboy asking the prom queen for a dance. Eric rubbed the back of his neck, trying to understand what she was saying.

When he couldn't, he gave up and asked, "Monica? What are you talking about?" He took great pains to stay away from that woman at all costs. Understanding hit him. "Wait a minute. Is this about what she said that day at your shop when you crowned her with chocolate? Hinting that she and I were dating? She is not, never has been, and will *never* be my girlfriend. I feel like I should wear a string of garlic around my neck whenever she's near."

"You left so quickly after her, it looked like you were together."

"I wanted to laugh out loud when you dumped chocolate on her. She deserved it. I left because you looked like you wanted to throw chocolate on me next. By the way, I didn't agree with her comment about you needing to hit the gym." He let his gaze travel the length of Ann's curvy figure. "You have a fantastic body in my opinion." *I can't believe I said that out loud.*

Their gazes locked, and Eric felt that same slow burn in his gut that always started when he was around Ann. He'd been in love with her for as long as his heart had beat, but it was useless. Though she looked at him, she never really saw him. For reasons he'd never figured out, she'd taken a dislike to him in high school. To her, he was her enemy. They couldn't agree on anything. Last month they'd both volunteered to help decorate the high school gym for a dance, and by the end of the night, they'd been at war.

With what that jerk of a fiancé had done to her and now Lewis, the last thing she'd be interested in was another man. He'd have to continue pretending that he didn't feel a damn thing for her. Otherwise, she'd turn and run. But maybe she'd be able to see him if she could just get to know him.

"Why do you want to date me?" Ann asked.

"I don't actually want you to date me. I thought we could help each other out. You need me, and I need you." Eric winced as he admitted, "I need help leaving behind the nerd in me." He was somewhat satisfied with his appearance, but he knew he had nerdish tendencies that sometimes morphed into full-blown goofiness. Ann could help him become the kind of confident, suave guy women like her were attracted to. In the process, this was a golden opportunity for them to change the dynamic of their relationship. *No way am I going to walk away from this.*

"The nerd in you?" She looked him up and down, then frowned. "I don't understand. You're not talking about actually dating, then, right?" She chewed her lip.

Only in my dreams.

"No, I just need you to make me the kind of guy you'd *want* to date. Look, it's true that the good guys, who are often the nerds, end up in the friend zone. They're not the guys women pick. I want to go from nerd to bad boy. And you can show me how. I need help with everything from choosing clothes to all things related to dating."

"I don't know," she said, eyeing him with disapproval.

Feeling like he was losing the potential for her help, he pushed on. "Helping me won't take up much of your time. It'll take a couple of weeks, tops." He grinned. "Unless I'm more of a nerd than I think I am." His smile faded when she didn't respond right away. Did she think he was too much of a dork?

"I don't know, Eric. I thought I'd be able to pay you at least something, and I don't want to feel like I'm the one doing all the benefiting."

"It wouldn't be like that." He touched the documents she'd brought to him. "Winning your case will help me gain favor with the firm and hopefully get that partnership I'm after."

"I didn't realize that you'd left your own practice, or I never would have come to you."

Eric was glad that she hadn't known. He wouldn't have wanted to miss this chance to help her. "They made me an offer that I couldn't refuse." His father had refused to pay for his mother's rehab treatment, which had left the expense to fall on Eric's shoulders. Though he'd made enough to take care of his own bills with his practice, it wasn't enough for her medical needs, so he'd had to give it up. But he wasn't about to tell Ann any of that. He didn't want her to feel sorry for him. "Plus, they gave me a steady client right away. Have you heard of the Thompson Corporation?"

Ann nodded, her eyes widening. "Who hasn't? They're behind all those commercials where they say they're in the business of putting the romance back into relationships. Going to one of their retreats is all the rage in Hollywood right now."

"Exactly, they're a pretty big deal. So, when I say that I can afford to take your case without charging you, I mean it. You just turn this frog into a prince, and we'll call it even."

"It would mean spending a lot of time together."

Hearing the doubt in her voice, Eric rushed to say, "We'll have to do that anyway for the case."

Ann stared at him, then made a "turn around" motion with her finger.

He complied, then held his arms out. "Well? What's the verdict?"

"I think I can help you."

Eric hoped so. If he was going to get Ann to see him as the kind of guy who was right for her, he needed the help. It wasn't until recently that he'd finally picked up a clue as to why Ann had never been interested in him. Eric could still remember the words of the last woman he'd dated.

She'd called him a nice guy, a good man, and at the time Eric hadn't cared. He *was* a good guy, and what was wrong with being that kind of man? Someone with integrity and courage, who didn't use women. But then it had clicked that maybe the reason Ann had never given him the time of day was because he was nothing like Lewis or any of the slack-jawed weasels she'd dated. Not that he wanted to be a slack-jawed weasel. He simply didn't want to be the nerd any more.

Aware that Ann was staring at him, he said, "What?"

"I don't know. Maybe I shouldn't do this." Indecision crossed her face. "There's so much tension between us because…" her voice trailed off.

Eric got the impression that what she hadn't said was something he wouldn't like. "Don't stop now."

"We don't really get along. That could cause problems." For some reason, a flash of hurt crossed her face when her gaze roamed his chest, then she darted her focus back up to meet his eyes. Clenching her hands into fists and breathing faster, she said, "We're too different, and spending time together could end in disaster."

"The past is the past. You're a client to me. Nothing more." *If only that were true.* "I only want you to make me over. That's it." Hiding the disappointment coursing through him when she didn't immediately agree, he waited for her to walk off the way she usually did whenever they were in the same room together for longer than a few minutes. To his surprise, she didn't.

She studied him for a second. "Is the bad boy transformation to help you land a specific woman?"

He raised his eyebrows. "No." He went on, not wanting to hear her say anything that might sting, "I only want you to help me change, give me some pointers. Basic stuff, nothing earth shattering. What do you say?"

Her brow furrowed before she sighed. "I don't have the luxury of refusing. I can't afford to because I need your help, but I don't like the thought of a fake relationship. I want to make it clear that there's nothing between us and that we're not pretending to other people that there is."

He didn't blame Ann for that. Resorting to a fake relationship wasn't something he was interested in, either. He wanted the real thing or nothing.

"Agreed. I don't want to pretend there's anything going on that isn't."

Her relief was clearly visible. "We don't exactly get along that well. Do you honestly think we can work together?"

"I don't know, but I'm willing to try," he said.

She swept aside a strand of hair that fell. "I hate that our mutual need is pushing us together, because God knows, we'd never do something like this otherwise."

He caught another quick flash of hurt in her eyes and wished he knew what that was about. He wished he had the ability to wave his hand and erase all the pain she'd experienced. "Well? Are we in agreement or not?" He tapped the papers on his desk. "If you don't want to, then I recommend you get Ishmael James to take your case. He's a friend and a good attorney, and he might be willing to take the case pro bono."

Ann thought for a minute and still didn't look that sure, but extended her hand anyway. "I know that despite everything, you're a good attorney. So, a bad boy makeover in exchange for you keeping me out of the big house. It's a deal."

Despite everything? What was that supposed to mean? Too relieved that she'd agreed, he didn't dwell on what she'd said. Eric grasped her hand and smiled down at her. The jolt from the contact spread to his bones. It shouldn't have surprised him. This was Ann, the only woman he'd ever given his heart to. The day he'd realized she was the one had shocked him.

He'd always been more interested in science and math in high school than girls, determined to keep his mind on his studies, attend an Ivy League, and take the world by storm… until he'd seen Ann for the first time.

He'd swallowed his gum, choked, then raced for the water fountain, nearly mowing her over in the hallway of their high school. Science, math, and the future had all fallen off his radar once she'd entered the picture. They hadn't exactly been friends, but he'd managed to work up the nerve to say hi to her whenever he'd seen her. Then, for some reason, she'd stopped speaking to him, not even acknowledging him when he spoke. The only reason he could figure out was that she didn't want to lose popularity points by being seen talking to him. That had definitely wounded his pride.

It had taken him a while before he'd been able to regroup and regain his focus, but he had. Only because he'd wanted to finish college first before he approached her, this time as a success, he hoped. He'd planned to lay it all on the line and tell her how he'd always liked her. He'd fantasized that maybe the two of them could start dating while he was in law school, but when he'd stopped by her grandfather's house one evening, flowers and his heart in hand, he was too late. She'd been at her car, kissing her latest weasel. Eric had thrown away the flowers and gone to a bar with his friends Nick and Chad, to drink away his dashed hopes.

When Ann made a small noise of protest, Eric realized he was still holding her hand. Releasing his grip, he forced a smile that was far more relaxed than he felt and motioned to the phone. "I'll make some calls on your behalf. Why don't we meet tonight?"

"Okay, but don't wear your 'Home is where the Wi-Fi lives' T-shirt."

He grinned. "Too geeky, huh? All right. Let's meet at seven for dinner, and we can work out the details then."

“Good idea.” She held up her arms. “Maybe I can finish removing these handcuffs by then.”

Eric was about to suggest a place when he realized they were no longer alone.

“There you are, Ann! No wonder I couldn’t find you anywhere. Handcuffs? Really?”

At the sound of her grandfather’s voice, Ann sprang away from Eric, and he bit back a groan at the delight on the older man’s face. Noah Snyder was the biggest matchmaker in town. He’d made it clear before that he thought Eric and Ann belonged together. Based on his friends’ experiences with Noah, the older man was known to create a lot of havoc when he meddled. That wasn’t something Eric needed in his life ever, but especially not at the moment, not when he was trying to get Ann to see him differently. The last thing he wanted was for Ann to feel pushed at him. She’d balk and immediately run.

Twisting his fedora in his hands, Noah said, “I was looking all over for you, Ann. When Amelia called and told me what happened, I was worried. I wanted to find you to make sure that you were all right.”

“I’m fine, Granddaddy. Tell my sisters that it’s okay. Eric is taking the case.”

Noah’s thick gray eyebrows went skyward, and he stared at the handcuffs, then sent Eric an assessing look with steely eyes from beneath his white eyebrows. “Is that all he’s taking?”

“Yes, it is,” Ann said firmly and linked her arm through her grandfather’s. “Come on, I’ll walk you to your car.” Over her shoulder, she said, ”I’ll see you tonight, Eric.”

As soon as the door closed behind her, Eric sprang into action. From what he’d read in the documents Ann had given him, this situation could turn even uglier for her if he didn’t act fast. His father worked in the FDA’s Criminal Investigations Unit, so he knew how they worked. He would never ask his father for any favors with the case, though. Eric had grown up being told that he'd never amount to anything. He'd handle Ann's case on his own, win it, and prove his father wrong. Grabbing his phone, he started dialing.

Chapter Three

Outside Eric's law office, in the rain that was now only lightly falling, Ann stopped and looked around the parking lot, then shot a glance at her grandfather. "Where's your car?"

"Ran out of gas about a half mile back."

Narrowing her eyes, Ann said, "Then why aren't you wet?"

"Um..."

With a sigh, Ann guessed, "You had Henry drop you off, didn't you?" Henry was her grandfather's best friend and her sister Amelia's new grandfather-in-law.

"All right," Noah grumbled, "you caught me."

"This is one time that you really have to butt out of my life." Ann led the way to her car and unlocked it so he could get in. She shut the door, then walked around to the driver's side. "There's a lot at stake. Like my freedom if you screw things up." She put on her seatbelt and started the engine.

With a hand on his heart, Noah said, "When have I ever screwed anything up?"

"How about conniving to get Amelia and Chad to marry

at a wedding that turned out to be fake?"

"But they married for real in the end. Look how happy they both are," he argued.

Pulling out of the parking lot back onto Main Street, Ann drove toward her grandfather's house, taking care to avoid the deeper puddles of water. "Promise me that you won't do anything."

He gave her puppy dog eyes. "Ann, my heart aches that you would think ill of me."

"Promise me."

"Okay, I swear to you that I won't interfere." Leaning forward, Noah dug out his wallet and opened it. "Do you need some money? It can't be easy with the IRS having taken your accounts."

Suspicious, Ann said, "I haven't even told Amelia or Abby about that. How'd you know?" Shaking her head, Ann added, "Forget it. You've already been snooping, haven't you?"

"Wanting to take care of my granddaughters and make sure they end up happy before I push up daisies isn't snooping."

Ann navigated the street where her grandfather's house was located and pulled into the driveway. Shutting off the engine, she got out and walked around the car, taking calming breaths as she did. Her grandfather was in his seventies. Meddling in her and her sisters' lives was something he'd always done. He meant well, she knew that, but sometimes, he only made things worse. She had to make sure he knew what kind of trouble he could cause if he interfered now.

Opening the door, she helped him out and walked with him up the steps to his home. She planned to have a talk with him, then return to her place and try to take her mind off the awfulness of the day. A few funny movies and some ice cream later and maybe she could finally relax.

Her plans changed when her grandfather unlocked the door to the home she and her sisters had once lived in together and said in a sad, quiet voice, "I see you girls often, but it's not the same as you all living with me. Sometimes I think I hear laughter or the sound of one of you giggling. I turn around and no one is there. Wishful thinking on my part. I guess I get lonely."

Ann's heart squeezed, and she immediately said, "I'll call Ame and Abby and see if they can come over for lunch."

Her grandfather's demeanor brightened. "That'd be great." Whistling, he disappeared into his bedroom, saying he was going to get his slippers.

Ann pried off the handcuffs with one of her grandfather's tools, then changed into a pair of sweat pants and an old gardening T-shirt she'd left behind the last time she'd been over helping to clean out the garage. After she called her sisters and they agreed to lunch, she got busy in the kitchen, whipping up the Italian grilled sandwiches her grandfather loved. By the time she was making the third one, her sisters had arrived.

"Granddaddy's lonely. We should really do something," Ann whispered so Noah wouldn't overhear.

"I've asked him repeatedly to move in with me and Chad, but he refuses," Amelia said as she removed the iced tea pitcher from the refrigerator and bumped the door shut with her hip.

"I've told him he was welcome to live with me and Nick, but he said we needed our privacy," Abby said.

"Well, you're both newlyweds, so maybe that's why he said no. I'll ask him to move in with me, especially since there's no future husband on my horizon," Ann said.

"I believe you're in for a surprise in the husband department. I think you'd better check the Magic 8 ball again, Sis."

Ann laughed. When they were younger, they'd used an old Magic 8 ball they found in the attic to seek advice about boys and dating. She put the sandwiches onto plates, and her sisters carried them to the dining room table. "After what Lewis has done, trust me, there's no future husband, and no present boyfriend. There's no man in my life at all unless you count my newly acquired bad boy project."

Abby was in the process of taking glasses from a cabinet for the tea while Amelia gathered napkins. Both of them paused to stare at Ann, and Abby said, "What?"

"Since the IRS took all my money, I didn't have any to pay Eric to take my case. So, we agreed to a trade. He saves my hide, and while he's doing that, I'm going to give him a makeover."

"What do you mean the IRS took your money?" Abby asked.

Ann explained what she'd learned. Amelia put her hands on her hips. "Abby and I would have helped you out financially."

"That's okay, Sis. I'm good." Both her sisters were successful in their own right—Abby, as the owner of the family diner, and Amelia, as a photographer.

This mess had happened because she'd blindly trusted someone she shouldn't have. She'd dig herself out of the business mess with Eric's help. She grimaced at the thought. If she and Eric could manage to spend time together without butting heads, it would be a miracle.

She was still mulling over the idea when Abby nudged her.

"So how much of a bad boy are you going to help turn him into?"

"Take him dancing and share a hot kiss or two and tell him it's part of the lesson plan," Amelia teased.

"It's not going to be anything like that. I don't think about him like that. Ever." *Except for this afternoon…* Ann ducked her head, sure that when it came to hot kisses, she was the last girl he had in mind.

"He's such a nice guy. I don't understand why you don't like him," Abby protested.

Ann had never shared the reason why she didn't care for Eric. She didn't like talking about it. To hear someone else say out loud the thoughts she'd had about herself hadn't been pleasant. "He's not the kind of guy I'd be interested in."

"You say that about him now. The next thing you know, you'll be getting married."

Amelia started humming the "Wedding March."

"Who's getting married?" Noah asked as he joined them at the table.

"Ann. She's going to give Eric a bad boy makeover, and she'll end up as his girlfriend."

Ann shot an exasperated look Abby's way and mouthed at her to stop.

Her grandfather laughed. "That relationship sure took off fast. From handcuffs to a wedding."

"Ha ha. Funny, but I'm doing this solely because Eric is going to keep the steel bracelets away. Since I can't pay him, I want to do something to help him in return."

"We told her we could help out financially," Amelia said.

Noah seated himself and took a bite of his sandwich. He chewed for a second, then offered softly, "I have some savings."

"Thanks, Granddaddy, but no." Ann squeezed his hand. Since the death of her parents when she was fifteen, he'd always been there for her, and it made her heart hurt to think of him being lonely. "I have an idea that I want to run by you. What would you think of moving into my place?"

"Not much," Noah said. "I'd keep you awake with all my partying."

The sisters laughed.

"Do you mean matchmaking?" Amelia said.

"Potato, potahto." Noah grinned widely at them. "Thank you for the offer, my dear, but I'm far too set in my ways to move in with someone else. I like my independence and being able to do what I want when I want."

"Doing what you want means keeping your word to me, right? You're going to butt out of my situation." There were so many things that could go wrong already. "I don't need you meddling."

"I said I'd keep my word, didn't I?" Noah gave her a bright smile.

Ann exchanged a look with her sisters. Hadn't her grandfather made the same promise to them?

"I won't breathe a word of your torrid love affair with Eric to another soul, I promise." Noah crossed his heart with his finger.

Ann sighed. "There's no torrid affair. We're just two people who are helping each other out."

"I get it. You're being neighborly. Like borrowing a cup of sugar."

Ann didn't like the expression on her granddaddy's face. The one that said he was trying too hard to look innocent.

He tapped the side of his glass and quirked an eyebrow at her. "Whatever came of that Dickson guy you had some classes with in college? I really liked him, and he would have made a great husband."

Ann rubbed the side of her forehead. "There were two major things wrong with him."

"Are you sure that it wasn't you being picky?"

"I'm sure. First, we never dated. Second, he never even asked me to date him, much less marry him. I can't imagine why considering the fact that he had a *girlfriend*."

"Details." Noah rubbed his chin. "Hmmm. What about that professor I met?"

"My English professor was sixty-something years old.

Granddaddy…listen." Ann patted his weathered hand. "I know you want me to be with someone, but I'm happy being single, okay?"

Noah jutted his chin out and nodded.

"That means no Eric, got it?"

He sent her a sly smile. "If I hadn't walked into his office when I did, who knows what I would have interrupted."

Ann sighed and gave up, letting her grandfather continue to ramble on about the list of eligible men she was missing out on. She was thankful when the meal finally ended. After she cleared the table, Ann helped rinse the dishes and then decided she'd go to her shop to see what kind of damage had occurred during the search. With the cease and desist order, she was afraid to open up business as usual. She wanted to check with Eric first to see if that was even feasible.

"I can meet you over there in about fifteen minutes and help you go through the shop," Abby said. "I already rearranged my schedule so that Nick is handling the diner the rest of the day. He needs the keys to be able to lock up, so I'll drop those off, then meet you at your shop."

"I can meet you after my doctor's appointment." Amelia nudged her. "Save me some chocolate."

"I'll do that, and whenever you guys can make it, that's fine. If you can't, it's not a big deal," Ann said, but she knew they'd be there for her. Through the ups and downs of life, her sisters had always offered their unflagging support. Ann knew how lucky she was. Not everyone had what she had. She hugged her sisters and Noah and promised to call to check in on him later that evening.

Heading out to her car, she dialed Eric's office number, and when he answered, she said in a deliberately husky voice, "What are you wearing?"

…

Eric dropped the stack of mail he'd been carrying, and the envelopes scattered across the hardwood floor. Ann's sexy tone had created all sorts of scenarios in his mind. "Do you always call someone like you're working a 900 number?"

"Just want to make sure that you don't wear that T-shirt. Or any of your other computer-speak ones."

Laughing, he said, "I won't," then asked, "Is something wrong?"

"I'm heading over to the shop to survey the search warrant damage."

"There shouldn't be too much, if any. Let me know if there is. The search warrant only allowed them to look for specific information, not go through everything."

"Okay. Am I allowed to open the shop back up for business?"

He hated to be the bearer of bad news. "There's nothing that explicitly prohibits you from opening, just from selling the supplements, but you're going to find it pretty difficult to run the shop without having the ability to pay your suppliers and other costs."

Her sigh was loud and clear. "I didn't think about that part. That would be a problem. Have you heard anything yet about me needing to get ready for shackles?"

"The legal process doesn't work that fast. I've made a few calls, and I'm waiting to hear back. You'll know the minute I know something. About dinner—do you want to go somewhere where jeans are appropriate or a suit and tie?"

"A bad boy doesn't ask. He does what he wants."

"And women like that sort of thing? What's wrong with being considerate and asking where she'd like to go?" What the hell kind of experiences did Ann have? He didn't agree with her on this point.

"They like confidence. I'm only telling you how it is."

"I don't know that I can deliberately act like a jerk, Ann."

"It's not about acting. A bad boy is something the guy is, not something he puts on."

"Okay, fine. I'll choose a place. A nice one."

"I'll make sure to wear a nice dress. Text me the address once you know where we're meeting." Ann said good-bye and hung up.

He thought about the last time he'd seen Ann in a nice dress. He hadn't known at the time all the heartache she'd faced with losing her parents in a car accident. He'd wanted to tell her how sorry he was, but they weren't friends, and he wasn't sure how to approach her. Later that year, when he'd heard that she wasn't attending the prom because her family's diner was going through a rough period financially, he'd spent his own money and shipped a prom dress to her home.

She'd shown up at the prom in the dress, with her friends and an idiot he knew wasn't good enough for her, but at least the idiot had had the nerve to ask her. A mistake Eric had always regretted. He'd never been able to work up the courage to tell her that he liked her. Then life had happened, and he and Ann had ended up at odds with one another. Now that another chance had landed in his lap, he wasn't going to blow it.

The door to his office opened. Eric turned from his thoughts to see who'd entered, and his day went from good to bad. It was his father, the one man who could set him on edge faster than anyone else. No one could live up to Ralph Maxwell's expectations, least of all Eric.

"I understand you're going to be the attorney on the Snyder case." He shook his head. "That's a bad career move. You don't want to gain a reputation as the man who defends criminals who steal hope from sick people."

"Ann isn't a criminal, and she's not guilty."

Ralph cast a critical eye around the office, and his lips thinned. "That's what they all say. Be smart this time."

"You're not lead man on the investigation. I already checked. So there's no conflict with me taking her case."

"Our family can't afford for there to be a hint of anything distasteful associated with our name. You know that."

Politics was in the family blood on his mother's side, and Eric's brother planned to run for governor. He and his siblings had grown up making sure the world never saw behind closed doors, never knew the secrets in the family. The few secrets that had managed to escape had been covered with a few well-placed lies. That's why his mother's alcohol rehab stint had been spun into a "treatment for exhaustion." Eric had no desire or intention to live wearing one mask for the public and another in private.

"I'm not part of that world anymore," Eric said quietly. He'd never regretted walking away from the immense wealth of his childhood, even though it'd meant he'd been cut off from the rest of the family. He'd left behind a hefty college fund, an inheritance, and a life already laid out for him from cradle to grave. He had no interest in politics. Rather than take an all expenses paid education at a prestigious private college handpicked by his father, he'd put himself through state college and then law school with hard work and loans.

Young and idealistic, he'd wanted to protect people from those who'd take advantage of them. Now that he was older, he wasn't so idealistic, but he'd never lost the desire to fight for people who were often the underdogs.

"You might think you're not, but you'll always be a Maxwell, and as such you have responsibilities to uphold." His father's voice continued to rise. "Taking this case could cast a pall over your brother's future campaign. When the dirt is uncovered, you can bet some of it will land on you, which will impact the rest of us."

Same song, different dance, and Eric was tired of his father attempting to manipulate him. "I thought I managed to make it pretty clear in the past that you can't force me to do what you want."

"You're making a mistake."

"It's mine to make."

Looking irritated, his father cleared his throat. "The family will stay at Martha's Vineyard next month for Thanksgiving. You need to be there this year."

"Can't make it." Besides the fact that he couldn't stand being around his father, he didn't particularly want to be stuck with the rest of the family, either. The gatherings always centered on whichever family member's latest political ambition needed help. Or which scandal needed to be covered up. After that, there was usually a round or two of arguing and backstabbing followed by seething covered under a veneer of politeness. Not a lot to be thankful for that was for sure.

"Your mother needs you."

Eric gritted his teeth, unable to withstand that trump card. His mother's battle with addiction made her health seem worse each time he saw her. "Fine, but you'll stay the hell out of my way."

Ralph straightened his tie. "I'll show myself out."

The easiest thing for Eric to do would be for him to use his father—and his connections—to make the case against Ann go away. But his father would never let him forget that Eric had needed him. Plus, Eric wanted to prove that he could win. In the process, he'd at least have a shot with Ann.

Chapter Four

Once she reached the shop, Ann stayed in the car to take a minute to gather her thoughts. She'd always felt lacking when compared to her beautiful sisters, like she was a beat out of step. Of the three of them, she was plainer, not as successful, and her love life often played out like an episode of *The Twilight Zone*. She'd never envied her sisters their beauty, their success, or the fact that they were both so crazy in love with two great men.

She just wanted to be good at *something*. That's why her business meant so much to her. When she'd created the gourmet truffles and sales had taken off, she'd thought—and hoped—that finally, maybe finally, she'd found her place. Landing the contract with a high-end store in New York that had agreed to carry some of her truffles, Ann had dared to let herself dream. Only now, that dream had been raided, and her life was hitting rock bottom.

Not only was she effectively out of business, but she was looking at some frightening legal trouble and having to accept help from the one man she'd rather not. She stiffened her shoulders. *Suck it up, buttercup*. She'd had a few hours of whining and giving in to the fear. Now she was done feeling sorry for herself. Life wasn't for wimps. She'd get over this somehow, because whatever other shortcomings she might have, one thing she had going for her was tenacity. So life had knocked her squarely on her "chocolate twenty" butt. She'd get back up and try again.

Pushing open the door of her Volkswagen, Ann stepped out. She unlocked her shop, hating the big closed sign on the door, but promised herself that it wouldn't be there long. Inside the cheerfully decorated space, the scent of chocolate lingered in the air, the smell stirring Ann's senses.

When her foot slid on something, Ann glanced down at the floor. Dozens of papers littered the ground. They were invoices for orders already paid for and some for orders pending. She'd need to make calls to explain the cancellation and figure out a way to refund the money to the buyers since she couldn't access her accounts.

Stooping, she picked up the invoices and placed them on the counter. How could Lewis do this to her? How could she have let herself get suckered by him? She'd thought they had an easygoing relationship built on mutual friendship and trust. After dating and trusting a string of bad boys, Lewis was the final straw for her. No more men in her life.

Reaching across the counter, she set the phone in front of her and dialed Lewis again. She got the same no longer in service message as before. Hanging up, she drummed her fingertips on the counter. Both of his elderly parents lived out on one of the islands. She planned to stop by their house and gently inquire about his whereabouts. Then she'd not so gently kick his butt if she caught up to him.

Ann put a hand up to her forehead, analyzing how she could escape the nightmare. What was going to happen to her reputation once all this became public? And what about those poor people Lewis had swindled? Were any of them struggling financially now because of what Lewis had done? The thought troubled her. She'd fix this for those people, whatever she had to do to come up with the money.

The bell on the door sounded, and Ann turned to find her sister entering.

Amelia put a hand to her lips as she surveyed the shop. "Oh, Sis. What can I do?"

"I'm only going to straighten up. There's not a lot more that can be done."

The door opened again, and Abby stepped in. "Wow." She set an iPod dock on the counter, cranked up some music, and clapped her hands together. "Let's get started. We'll have this cleaned up in no time. I solemnly swear that I will box up the chocolates and not eat a single one." Abby held up a hand with her fingers crossed.

Ann laughed. "You might as well help yourself to some since I can't open for business."

Abby dropped her purse onto a chair and regarded her sister. "I know things look bleak right now, but it will get better. For what it's worth, I never liked Lewis. I should have said something."

"I don't know that I would have listened. I trusted him, Abby. I thought he was my friend. How do I always attract men into my life who are either cheaters or jerks?"

"Because none of them are Eric?"

Ann rolled her eyes. "Anyway…it's too late to look back now. I can only go forward with this awful hand I've been dealt."

Abby picked up a bag and shook it out, then headed to the display case to choose an assortment of truffles. When she was done, she closed the bag and folded the top. "Don't you remember my own life? How bad things were at one point?"

"I do, and I'll get over this, I know it. Even laugh about

it one day. Maybe when I'm drunk or highly medicated, but I'll laugh. For now, this Cinderella needs to go to the ball, or rather dinner with Eric. I feel and look like one of the stepsisters right now." Ann gathered up some of the bags that had fallen on the floor and tossed them into the garbage can.

"I love this song," Amelia said and started dancing. "Come on." She grabbed Ann's hand and twirled her around, then Abby joined in, and the three of them shimmied and spun in the middle of the floor. Anyone looking in would have thought they'd all gone crazy. As they danced, Abby said, "Remember when Amelia put those Velcro mitts on her feet and tried to run across the living room rug?"

Ann laughed. The rug had stuck to the bottoms of the mitts, jerking Amelia to her knees and rolling her up like a burrito.

Amelia made a face. "I was little."

Ann danced with her sisters and laughed until her sides ached. Her phone vibrated with an incoming text, and she checked it. *Sunset Pier.*

She texted Eric back, and when she looked at her sisters, they were both smiling. "What?"

"I think it's time to get Cinderella ready for the ball," Amelia said.

Abby linked her arm with Ann's. "She's right. Come on, Cinderella, I'm buying you a new dress and shoes for your dinner tonight. I'll spring for a visit to the hair salon, too."

"Oh, no, I can't let you do that."

"Yes, you can," Abby insisted as she grabbed her purse. "You've always been there for me, helping and nagging the hell out of me even when I said I didn't need it, so it's my turn to return the favor."

"When have you ever *not* needed my nagging, hmm?"

Abby grinned. "If not for that talk you gave me when I was renovating the building to expand the diner, I might have missed what a great guy Nick is."

"If this is going to get newlywed mushy, I'm out of here. Lately you two could be the poster couple for a Hallmark movie."

Abby elbowed her gently. "I can't wait until you're in love. I never thought finding the right man after such a wrong one would happen for me."

"Is this where you break into song?" Ann teased.

"Once you're in love, you'll see what I mean." Abby stopped. "Wouldn't it be great if Eric turned out to be the one for you? Like a knight in shining armor, he rescues your business, and you fall in love with him."

"First, no. Second, no."

"Come on. Eric's nice, he's attractive, and he likes you," Amelia said.

"He's not that nice. And, okay, I'll give you the attractive part, but trust me when I say he doesn't like me and it wouldn't matter if he did. My that-guy's-a-jerk radar is busted. I'm not about to risk making yet another stupid mistake by trusting a man again. I'm done."

"I said the same thing, didn't I, Ame?" When Amelia nodded, Abby looked back at Ann in triumph. "See?"

"Yes, but this is different."

"I believe you."

Ann sighed. It was clear that her sister was placating her. "Once I help make over Eric and he slays my legal dragons, we'll part ways."

"Of course." Abby pulled out her cell phone. "Sure, okay. I'll get an appointment with the hair salon."

Ann resisted. "I should stay here and finish loading up the chocolates. I need to clean the place and then send out some business emails as well as make some calls."

"Do it another time, and we'll be here to help you again." Abby gave Ann a gentle push in the middle of her back.

"Right now I'm being the older, bossy sister."

"So what else is new?" Ann said with a laugh and allowed her sisters to prod her out of the shop. She locked up and climbed into the car with her sisters. Normally, she'd stay and do what needed to be done. But in the back of her mind was the thought that if she stayed and finished closing up, then it would signify the complete end of her business. She wasn't ready to let go yet.

• • •

Eric rose from his seat when the hostess led Ann to the table. The chatter of the other patrons, the clattering of silverware, the soft music, all of it disappeared as Ann walked toward him.

The emerald green dress flowed down the length of her body, accentuating each glorious curve, the hem stopping just above her knees, drawing attention to her long legs. On her feet, she wore a pair of shoes that were sexier than anything he'd ever seen her wear. And her hair fell in waves around her face… Her makeup… She looked… He swallowed. He'd always known she was beautiful, but tonight, she looked stunning. Mysterious. Mesmerizing. A siren calling him to crash on the rocks. And crash he would if he put action to the direction of his thoughts. Moving too fast might scare her off.

He pulled out a chair for her, and her perfume, a tantalizing floral scent that disturbed his peace of mind, wafted in the air. Pushing the chair forward as soon as she sat, he quickly returned to his own seat, praying that he'd be able to keep his mind on what she was saying rather than stare at her lips. But with Ann sitting close beside him with her full lips coated with a kiss-me-now red color, he'd be lucky if he didn't act like an idiot.

Once again, when he was around her, he acted as awkward

as he had back in high school. Unlike him, Ann appeared at ease. She smiled at the waitress and placed her order, then turned to look at him. Eric managed to act a lot smoother than he felt when he gave his order, then passed the menus back. Ann leaned across the table.

"Why did you pick this place?"

The way she leaned brought her lips into closer proximity, and Eric clenched his jaw. "Because it had a four and a half star rating on the Romantic Restaurants website."

Ann smoothed her hand down the side of her neck, and Eric's gaze followed the move.

"Bad idea for me to do that?"

"No, not at all." She bit her lip and shook her head, then searched her purse and pulled out a notepad and a pen. "While we wait for the food, we can get started on some things you can work on."

"I want you to be honest. Brutally so if you need to. I'm willing to do whatever it takes." Anything to get her to really see him.

She toyed with her earring. "Are you sure this is really what you want? You don't look too happy about all this."

He wanted her, and if he didn't look happy, it was only because he was afraid of messing up. Eric shook off his thoughts. "Yes, I'm serious. Sorry, I was lost in thought for a second there. Go ahead. Hit me. What's the first thing you noticed about me?" Her cheeks flushed. Maybe she was too warm.

"Okay." She tapped the end of the pen against his tie. "If you wear a tie, don't wear one like that."

Puzzled, Eric caught the end of his tie and looked down at it. "What's wrong with my tie?"

"The design looks like it's a series of controllers for video games."

"It is. If you look closely, the design is images of every

controller since the first one was—" He caught her expression and grinned. "Ah. I get it. Not very sexy, is it?"

"Honestly? No."

He leaned back when the waitress set their beverages on the table. As soon as the woman walked off, he said, "My suit?"

"Nice. Expensive. Very Wall Street."

"I get what you're not saying, but I can't exactly wear a leather jacket when I'm representing a client in court," he pointed out.

Ann shook her head. "Being a bad boy isn't simply about a leather jacket or owning a motorcycle. Those types of guys have a confidence in who they are. They're handsome, cocky, and," she shrugged, "to a lot of women, they represent a challenge."

He frowned. "Women really prefer a man who's a cocky challenge? Are you speaking personally?"

It was her turn to frown. "At the moment, I prefer no men at all."

Eric's heart sank. He could be faced with a losing battle if Ann had her mind and her heart closed to a relationship.

He glanced over at a couple seated near them when the woman let out a squeal. A proposal. When the woman threw her arms around the man's neck and they kissed, Eric glanced at Ann, not surprised to see how tightly her jaw was clenched. He wondered what it would be like if the two of them were ever locked in an embrace. Kissing.

Trying to focus his attention on his plan to win Ann over, he said, "Okay, step one, ditch the dork tie. What should I do about the suit?"

"You can rock a suit simply by buying one that's not so…1950. Don't worry. Later, I'll pull up some pictures online and show you what I mean. Okay…pants. Any casual pants you wear shouldn't be too loose. No billowing, no pleats.

Those make a man look heavier and frumpier. Think lean when it comes to buying pants. Shirts shouldn't be too large, otherwise, you— What?"

"I may need to go clothes shopping. What were you saying about the shirt?"

She leaned closer and brushed aside one end of his suit jacket. Tugging against the side of his shirt, she said, "If there's room to gather this much material in your hand, the shirt isn't right for you."

The way she'd angled her body put her face in line with his shoulder. She was so close, that when he glanced down, he could see how beautiful her eyes were. She stared at him one breath, two breaths, then three before she straightened back up. Again with the flush on her face.

"Then I'll definitely have to buy some new things. It would probably help if you came with me."

Her expression was slightly suspicious. "How do you normally choose your outfits?"

"I order them online. Usually two or three of the same kind if I like it."

Ann scribbled something in the notebook. "I'll try to fit you into my busy prison-avoiding schedule."

"Hey." He couldn't help himself. He reached across the table and covered her hand with his. "I'm not going to let that happen. I won't let you see the inside of a jail cell much less prison."

Her smile was dazzling. "You think so?"

Maybe he was being a bit too prideful when he nodded, but despite his father's constant put-downs over his choice of a career, he knew he was good at the law. He loved it. It was a way to right wrongs, a way to give justice to victims in a world that was often so lacking in it.

"After the clothes, we'll take a look at your other areas."

That brought Eric up short. "My other areas?" What else

was there besides a few changes in his wardrobe?

"Accessories—"

"I'm not about to put my wallet on a chain big enough to use as a jump rope."

She laughed. "I was referring to things like jewelry. An earring is a personal choice for a man. Bracelets can be cool depending on what they are. A belly button ring on a man is a very bad boy thing to do. You should get one."

"A *belly button* ring?" Eric lowered his voice when he realized he'd spoken so loudly he'd attracted attention.

Ann laughed again. "I was joking. A belly button ring on a guy is definitely anti-bad boy. At least, in my opinion."

"I hope you were joking. No way am I getting anything below the waist pierced. Or above it for that matter." He sighed. "Maybe I'm destined to be the guy next door. The dependable, sincere one."

"There's nothing wrong with that guy, Eric. The boy next door can be nice."

"Nice? Sure. Except that you—" He stopped himself in time. He'd almost said, "except that you don't want a nice guy." Instead, he amended it to, "know that most women don't want the nice guy. There's a reason they finish last."

She sipped some of her drink, then set the glass down carefully. "The boy next door can be the right guy. Very sexy." Her eyes widened, then she stammered, "I'm speaking in general. Not that I'm flirting with you when I say that."

"Yeah." Message received. He sighed and after their meals were delivered, switched the topic to something that was less personal. After they were finished and he paid, he suggested they take a walk in the park.

They headed out the side door that led to a small outdoor eating area that was empty thanks to the chill in the air. Iron tables and chairs were placed strategically around a small pineapple water fountain that led out to the sidewalk. Ann shivered in the chilly wind, and Eric took off his jacket and draped it around her shoulders. When she looked up at him, he said, "I don't care if that was a nerd move. You were cold, and I could do something about it."

She clutched the ends of the jacket and stared up at him, mouth slightly parted. "It wasn't a nerd move. It was thoughtful. Thank you."

"The boy next door, right?" He brushed her hair away from the collar of the jacket, then realizing what he was doing, quickly drew his hand away. "You sure you're up for a walk in the park?"

Her eyes sparkled. "I love walking when the fall leaves are on the ground. It's one of my favorite things to do. What about you? Do you have a favorite thing to do?"

He lifted his shoulders in a shrug. "Besides buying ties with nerd designs?" She laughed, and he continued, "I enjoy traveling. I've been to several countries over the years."

She snuggled farther into his jacket as they walked past the bustling restaurants, bars, and groups of local college kids. "I love traveling, too, but I hate doing it alone."

"I can imagine. As a beautiful woman, you're probably subject to a lot of pickup attempts when you're by yourself." He didn't know what he'd said wrong, but her smile faded and the mood changed.

She cleared her throat and glanced at her watch. "We'd better make it a quick stroll." When she stepped onto the grass, her foot slid a little on a gathering of leaves.

Eric instinctively reached out his arm to help her. "You okay?"

"Fine."

He knew she wasn't being completely honest with him, but for the life of him, he didn't know what he'd done wrong. He only knew he wanted to figure it out so he could fix it. When he was dealing with any other client, he'd simply ask questions until he knew what was going on. But with Ann, he had a feeling that he might not like the answer she gave him. What if what was troubling her was about another guy? Did he really want to hear that? He didn't mind being her shoulder to lean on if that's what she needed, but he wanted to be careful he didn't end up in the friend zone. He'd seen it happen before. He didn't want to end up like his college buddy. Watching the girl he liked marry someone else all because he hadn't taken the chance, hadn't stepped up and told her how he'd felt. Eric had to take a chance. Make it clear to Ann that he was here for her, but he didn't want to ever become her crying-over-other-men pal.

As they walked up the steps leading into the gazebo, he blurted out, "I don't want to be friends."

• • •

Ann silently seethed. "I don't think you have to worry about that happening."

A look crossed his face. Dismay? "What I meant was—"

She cut him off with a wave of her hand. "I'm your client. You're my...whatever you want to label this makeover project, and that's all this is." Ann turned away from him and looked out across the grounds. The look on his face. Like she was trying to become his friend so she could jump him or something. As if.

A clear image of the glimpse she'd caught of his muscles played in her mind's eye, and she took a deep breath. When Eric's arm brushed against hers, she shivered, but this time, it wasn't because of the wind. She glanced up to see him looking down at her. He'd always had such soulful eyes. She looked away.

"Ann, I get tongue-tied sometimes. I don't know why. I'm not someone who's shy."

"Then it's me. You don't know what to say around me."

He nodded.

"I understand." He wanted to make sure she didn't have anything romantic on her mind when it came to him but didn't know how to say it. She'd clear that up right now. "Don't worry, we don't have to be friends."

"No, I *do* want to be friends." He groaned when he said it and smacked his forehead with the heel of his hand.

Ann swallowed. Pity friendship? No, thanks. He probably felt sorry for her because of her legal troubles. "Listen, Eric, it's okay. I have no intentions toward you other than your professional abilities. Anything more would take the focus off my case and it's better that we don't have the distraction or the pretense that we like each other enough to be friends."

Why did he have to look like she'd slapped him? She could never understand what went on in a man's mind. Hadn't he made it clear since high school that he didn't want to be her friend? She turned away from him and started down the steps, and he caught up with her.

"The annual Halloween costume party is coming up. The prize money is up to about a hundred dollars for best costume. Are you planning on attending?"

She nodded. "I had my costume all picked out, but I'm not sure I'm going to wear that anymore. I was planning on going as a prisoner, which is why I had on the handcuffs that day in your office. I bought the costume a month ago, but it doesn't seem as funny now. Why?"

"Maybe you could save me a dance."

He didn't want to be her friend, but he wanted a dance? Whatever. When she reached the restaurant parking lot where she'd left her Volkswagen, Ann fumbled in her purse. She wanted to find her keys, drive home, and grab some ice cream. If she were as pretty and confident as her sisters, she'd be able to laugh and flirt with Eric and let bygones be bygones.

But she'd learned to put her guard up and use humor as her defense, because she wasn't pretty and she wasn't confident. "If you dance as well as you parallel park, no thanks."

Eric frowned for a second, then laughed. "It was my first time behind the wheel, and the driver's ed teacher didn't exactly tell me how to get it done."

"He was too busy flinching when he saw that garbage can you hit coming toward the passenger window."

"I was the only kid in the entire class to fail the driver's test. I was so humiliated. My father made me practice parallel parking seven days a week for three weeks after that. Failure isn't something a Maxwell does."

Ann couldn't imagine living with someone as strict and hard as she'd heard Eric's father was rumored to be. The end of her dress whipped up, wrapping itself around his leg, and he captured the material, holding it in his hand.

"Thanks." Ann gathered her dress in one hand and with the other, tried to get the key to work in the lock. After she'd tried a few times, he took the keys from her and slid them into the lock. His hand covering hers gave her the jolt she'd felt when he'd done the same at the restaurant.

"Do you want to continue our makeover conversation?" Though Ann wanted to run home and drown her insecurities in ice cream, maybe she shouldn't do that. The sooner she got him squared away as the bad boy he wanted to become, the less time she'd have to spend in his company and the less confusion she'd feel. "Yes, let's continue. Why don't we head to my place?"

"Okay, I'll follow you home."

Ann climbed behind the wheel and slid the key into the ignition, jumping in surprise when he leaned in. "Are you okay? I'm picking up a vibe that you're upset."

"Nope. I'm fine. I'll see you at my place." She kept the smile fixed on her face until he moved away and walked toward his car, then she exhaled. What was wrong with her? The last thing she needed was to feel uncertain and confused about Eric. The emotions magnified when she looked into those soulful eyes of his or when he touched her, and that wasn't good.

She lifted her gaze to the rearview mirror as he pulled out of the parking lot behind her. There was something about him that, despite her inner objections, pulled at her. And she was right to feel those objections. Knowing her past, the way she always ended up with a guy who was so wrong for her, was probably why she felt the pull. History kept repeating itself. Eric was definitely wrong for her. Not only had he proved in the past what kind of guy he was, but now he wanted this bad boy makeover, which was exactly the kind of guy she tried to avoid like a bad case of split ends.

Chapter Five

Eric's hands tightened on the wheel until his knuckles ached. Being in close proximity to Ann was harder than he'd thought it would be. When he'd leaned into her car, he'd almost given in to the urge to kiss her. That move wouldn't have earned him any points, though, that was for sure.

He couldn't believe how badly he'd botched the conversation about not being her friend, then fumbled over saying he wanted to be her friend. He sighed. When he spoke to other women, he never got tongue-tied. Never fumbled. Didn't act like an idiot. With them, he'd never had anything to lose. But with Ann, his heart was on the line, and he wanted to say all the right things, do all the right things. He wanted to impress her and sweep her off her feet. Instead, he'd ensconced himself squarely in the "we-aren't-friends" zone, which was worse than the friend zone. This was the no-way zone. The no-way guy was the one who couldn't make it through the I'd-date-him gate.

Giving himself a mental shake, he steered the car onto Ann's street. He'd try again. He couldn't let her think that he didn't want to be her friend. He simply didn't want to be *just* her friend.

The taillights of her car brightened as she braked and pulled into her driveway.

Eric climbed out of his car to follow Ann, determined to say the right words this time.

Once inside her house, she reached down to slide one high-heeled shoe off. Eric followed the curve of her leg as she slowly lowered it. His gaze slid to her other leg as she removed the second shoe, and he forgot everything he'd planned to say. She walked barefoot to a set of built-in shelves housing an iPhone dock. Setting her phone in it, she touched a few buttons, and soft music filled the room. "I like to have music playing. Helps me relax," she explained. "Do you want some coffee or something?"

An image of her long, shapely legs flashed through his mind. *Or something*. "No. I'm good." He motioned toward the dining room. "Okay if we sit at the table?"

"Sure." She went to an end table by the sofa to get a notebook and pen before leading the way to the dining room. "I want to keep the notebooks separate for your makeover. One is for clothing, the other will be for accessories, the third one for—"

"Hang on a second. How many notebooks do you think it's going to take?" It didn't bode well for her seeing him as dateable the more notebooks she brought out. He took a seat, expecting her to take one opposite him, but instead, she pulled out a chair right beside him. *Great*. That would help him concentrate on not blowing the conversation. *Not*.

Plopping the notebook down in front of her, she uncapped the pen, and studied him. "Haircut."

"What?"

"Your hair is longer than you normally wear it."

She'd noticed. He couldn't help but smile at that. "I've

been meaning to get to the barbershop."

"No, no." She ducked her head, toyed with the spirals on the notebook. "Longer hair on a man is sexy."

If Ann thought longer hair was sexy, he'd grow it to his ankles. "Okay." *Way to go, Eric. Sweeping her right off her feet with those scintillating one-word answers.*

Her gaze found his. "Plus, the longer style suits your bone structure and…" Her gaze swept across his chest, then back up to meet his eyes. "Um…build."

Eric ran his fingers through his hair. He hadn't missed the way she'd looked at him, and it made him want to pound his chest and let out a jungle yell.

She made a notation, then studied him again. "Try a five o'clock shadow. That's sexy on a man."

"You think that's sexy?"

Her slow smile made his mouth go dry. "I think that's *very* sexy." She blew out a breath, and he thought he saw her hands shake. Was she worried about offending him? She shouldn't be. He'd told her to be brutally honest if she needed to. "Hey." When she looked at him, he winked. "Go ahead and say whatever's on your mind."

"Let's talk about your clothes again." Her voice sounded breathless. "There's a lot to cover as far as clothing because of the different seasons. You don't want to look like a bad boy in the winter and then blow it in the summer by wearing something like socks with sandals."

"Even I know that's not something women find sexy."

"Right." She laughed and leaned close, dropping her voice. "So there's hope for you yet. You said you couldn't wear a leather jacket in court, and I get that, but that doesn't mean you can't any other time. Wearing a leather jacket is hot. I don't suppose you can ride a motorcycle."

"I can."

Her eyebrows shot upward. "I've never seen you on one."

"I wrecked it when I was eighteen. Wore that road rash like a badge of honor. I left it behind when I moved from my family's estate."

"Wow, who knew?" She made some notes and then tucked a strand of hair behind her ear.

The action gave him a better view of the side of her neck. *So tempting.*

Tapping the notebook with the tip of the pen, she looked at him. "Is there anything you want?"

What a loaded question. "I suppose in the course of this makeover you'll show me what women want the most from a date?"

Ann snapped her fingers like it was a great idea. "Yes, and I can teach you examples if we go to dinner, take in some movies, dance together."

"That sounds like real dating."

"Not at all," she said in what sounded like a hasty comeback to him. Ann closed the notebook and tapped the front of it. "For others maybe, but not us."

"Right, because you're not my type. We'd never date for real." He'd meant it to be a question but it came out sounding like a statement, almost like an insult, but he hadn't intended it to. Another screwup on his part. Before he could clarify, Ann reacted.

She put a hand over her chest. "You've broken my heart. How will I ever live through this rejection?"

Her easy dismissal stung. Giving her a tight smile, he said, "What else do I need to know?" She took a breath. "Okay. On to conversations. Be sugar, not artificial sweetener when you talk to women."

He blinked. "In English."

Ann tapped the notebook again. "Be real. Bad boys aren't the type of guys who fake stuff to interest a woman. For example, some guys will act like they're really in touch with their feminine side."

"Are you saying not to be sensitive?" Be sensitive. Don't be sensitive. How was a guy *ever* supposed to understand a woman?

"I'm saying don't be so sensitive that a woman thinks you could pass as her sister."

"Ooh. That's not a pretty mental image."

"Precisely."

Ann held up a finger in a warning gesture. "Always stick with the truth when you're having a conversation. You don't want to inflate yourself. The lies catch up with you."

"I'm an honest guy." She didn't respond with agreement, not that he'd expected her to, but he hoped she came to see that he wasn't the kind of man who'd hurt her.

"Let me get back to clothes." She gave him a critical once over. "You're tall and good looking, so you can pretty much wear anything when it comes to jeans. The better they fit, the better your body looks in them." His head was beginning to spin.

"Avoid jeans that are baggy. They make your thighs look big."

Eric rubbed the side of his face. "I don't care if my thighs look big."

She gave him a sweet smile. "Oops. Never mind. That's my issue. Um…let's see. Ah. Jeans. Stay away from butt-crack jeans, Bo Duke jeans, and dad jeans."

Eric shook his head. "So many things to watch out for. I think life is easier as a nerd."

"But you wanted this change, right?"

What he wanted was *her*. "Right. Go on."

"Okay…mesh T-shirts. No, no, double no." She held up her hand. "Wait. Hear that? I love this song!" Jumping to her feet, she wiggled her fingers. "Come on, let's dance. Dancing is something simple a bad boy can do on a date. And if you have trouble talking to women, dancing cuts down on conversation time."

Easy for her to say. She didn't have to desperately concentrate on something else. *He* was the one who could see her in that dress. The one who had to fight the electricity that sang along his nerve endings. Eric took her hand and slid his other one around her waist. He didn't have trouble talking to women. He had trouble talking to her, and holding her close wasn't going to make it any easier to have a conversation.

Eric fought the urge to put his hand against the flush on her face. Their bodies were within a hair's breadth of touching. He inhaled the intoxicating scent of her perfume as they moved. "You dance well," he said softly, desperate to keep a conversation going so he wouldn't do something stupid like press his lips against the side of her neck and continue lower until there was no going back.

"I took lessons. After our parents died, I thought I'd have to drop out because of finances but Abby managed to pull a rabbit out of a hat somehow, and I was able to keep taking them." She smiled up at him.

Eric knew that. He'd passed by the dance studio once and because it had been summer, the doors were open. He'd overheard a teenage Abby asking the instructor to please give her more time to pay Ann's bill. The minute Abby had left, he'd darted into the studio and paid for a year's worth of lessons with the stipulation that no one in the Snyder family ever know who'd taken care of the bill.

"How'd you learn to dance?"

Eric deliberately kept his eyes focused on a painting over her sofa rather than her. "Because I have three sisters, I grew up in the world of cotillion balls. Escorting debutantes was a pastime in my world and so was knowing the right dances."

She pulled back slightly to look at his face. "You don't sound like you were very fond of it."

"I wasn't. Though I was born into that world, I never felt like I belonged. As soon as I graduated high school, I got away from it all." He didn't want to go into detail about his mother, who'd worked so hard to create the facade of the wonderful, close-knit Maxwells when nothing could be further from the truth.

"You're not from here. How were you allowed to attend school in Sweet Creek?"

"My family is located mainly on some of the outer islands and in Charleston. I talked my way into staying with my mother's former nanny here so I could attend the high school. I had a couple of friends there, and I hated the private school I'd attended."

"You're not close to your family?"

"Not by a long shot." Eric knew that Ann didn't understand families that didn't love and support one another, because she'd had the opposite.

"I'm sorry."

The way that her lips were softly parted was more than he could stand, but he had to. He released his hold and abruptly stepped back to stride across the room and shut off the music. Walking backward toward the door, he said, "It's getting late, and I promised Nick I'd stop by. I'm going to go."

She looked a little surprise by his abruptness, and Eric knew it probably came across as rude, but he couldn't explain how holding her affected him. "I can come over to your place tomorrow, and we can get started on the next phase of operation bad boy," she offered.

When he groaned, she said, "Have you changed your mind?"

"Not at all. I'll call you then to see what time is good for you." He quickly left her bungalow and called himself twenty kinds of a fool. What had made him think he could be around her and keep his head clear? This whole bad boy project would come back to bite him if he wasn't careful.

Eric settled himself into his car. When he'd first suggested she help him, he'd thought it was a brilliant idea. Now, he wasn't so sure. It was hell being around her, pretending that she was nothing more than a client to him.

Driving through the streets toward Nick and Abby's house, Eric passed a house where a handful of children rushed out to greet a man. A woman followed behind, and the man spun her around in his arms. The laughter on their faces made Eric look away. He couldn't remember much, if any, laughter in his home growing up. Plenty of tension and competition. Plenty of making sure he looked good and didn't do anything to embarrass the family. To keep the peace, he'd gone along with the program until he'd graduated high school.

He could still remember the scathing words his father had hurled after him as Eric packed up only the clothes he'd paid for himself and walked out the door for the last time. The ugly words hadn't mattered to him because he had what he'd always wanted. Freedom. He could finally breathe when he'd distanced himself from that house.

Fifteen minutes later, Eric arrived at the home Nick had built himself and knocked on the door. Nick let him in and offered him a drink. Eric headed into the living room and settled in one of the matching recliners. Returning with a cold beer, Nick handed it over and sat in the other recliner.

The scent of something baking hung in the air. Eric sniffed appreciatively but declined when Ann's sister Abby came to greet him and offered him a piece of the brownie concoction.

"Better not. I just had dinner with Ann."

"Let me know if you want anything." She smiled at her husband, and Eric felt a pang of envy as he wondered if Ann would ever look at him that way.

Nick smiled. "How's it going?"

"Well, let's see. I told Ann that I didn't want to be her

friend."

Nick winced.

"Then I clarified that by putting myself in the friend zone."

"Ouch," Nick said. He clapped Eric on the shoulder. "The pursuit can be confusing, frustrating, and make you think it'd be easier to pound nails into cement with your thumb. But I'm telling you that loving and winning the heart of a Snyder woman is worth everything you'll go through."

Eric hesitated, then said, "My father's in the FDA unit that's investigating Ann. He's waiting for me to beg him for help to make her case go away, but I can't."

Nick raised his eyebrows and asked, "Why not?"

"Part of it's pride, part of it's that my father has always used his influence and wealth to sway people even when something wrong was going on. I don't want there to be any hint of a cover up on this case."

"I can understand that. It's better to be on the level. But have you considered the possibility of what might happen if you lose this fight?"

Eric had, and he didn't like where his thoughts had taken him. If he lost, Ann would pay for it. He didn't want to think about failing her. He pulled his briefcase onto his lap and opened it.

"I brought the will with the changes that you wanted, to make Abby your beneficiary. All you need to do is sign it."

Nick took the pen he offered. "How's Ann acting around you?"

"I can't read her. One minute she's laughing and joking and the next she's looking at me, and I feel a punch to the gut. I don't know."

Grinning, Nick said, "That about describes it. You never know how things will turn out. Look at Abby and me. We were never going to happen as a couple, and yet here we are."

Trying to get Nick away from discussing Ann, Eric asked, "How's the family? How's your brother?"

"My grandmother put her house in Texas on the market. She's planning to move to Sweet Creek to be closer to us." Nick's smile faded, and his face darkened. "Elliot and his wife are still separated. He's going through hell emotionally, but he's not used to letting anyone help him work through stuff."

"Sorry, man."

"Yeah." Nick took another swallow of the beer and reached for the paperwork. After he signed it, he said, "Are you going on the annual lake house trip this year? Everyone's going after the Halloween costume party."

"The whole family?"

"Ann, me and Abby, Amelia and Chad, and Noah and Henry."

Eric had always enjoyed staying at the lake house, but the few times he'd gone, Ann hadn't been there. He and the guys had spent time fishing, then challenged the women to boat races around the lake. They'd taken turns cooking food over the outdoor fire pit. Noah's barbecue ribs were legendary. Late at night, they'd all sit around the fire roasting marshmallows and sharing beers and stories. He'd loved feeling like part of the family. He wondered how different spending time at the lake would be if Ann were present.

Eric's phone buzzed with a text message, and he glanced at it. Ann had written: *Bad boys don't wear footie pajamas* followed by a yawning emoticon. Eric couldn't help laughing, and he responded with a simple *good night*. When he looked up, Nick was reading over his shoulder and grinning.

"What?"

"Ann is texting you good night along with little faces? You're already on your way to a tuxedo fitting, and you don't even know it."

Eric took the paperwork and shoved it back into his

briefcase, snapping it shut. "You know how I feel about Ann, but I don't think so. She's not even remotely interested."

"If that's your story. I have one request then."

"What?"

"I want to be the best man when you marry her. I'll throw you a bachelor party so wild that it'll end up on the news."

Eric finished off his beer and rose to leave. "Don't hold your breath. I'll file these in the morning. If you need anything else, let me know."

"You know I'm going to gloat when it happens."

"See you later, man." Eric left, then realized he was smiling. He had the kind of easygoing relationship with Nick that he'd always wanted with his own brothers. His smile faded. Nick was a great friend, but he was off the mark about Ann.

Eric was hoping she'd eventually turn to him, but he knew life didn't always work out the way someone wanted it to. He hoped spending time with her was a chance to win her heart. If getting Ann to see him as a romantic partner failed, he wasn't sure he could put himself out there again. He'd have to walk away. This time, for good.

Chapter Six

Later that evening, when Ann got ready for bed, she had a sinking feeling she was in over her head with Eric. As they'd danced, she'd been too aware of every movement of his body. That was a problem. She didn't want to think about Eric. About the feel of his hands. About how handsome—

Groaning, Ann rolled over and punched her pillow to fluff it up. Watching the shadows from a passing car play across the ceiling, she tried to keep her thoughts from swinging between Eric and her future.

With Eric handling the case, she didn't feel nearly as nervous as she had when she'd first learned the news. Maybe, just maybe, everything was going to turn out okay for her business. Her last thought before she drifted off to sleep turned out to be *so* wrong.

When the phone rang shortly after six the next morning, the sound jarred her awake. Worried that it was one of her sisters, she quickly leaned out of bed and grabbed the phone, mumbling a sleepy, "Hello."

She caught the irate words of "sue you" and "investment"

before she stammered out that the caller would need to speak with her attorney. After that, there was no way Ann could sleep. She showered, made herself some coffee, and sat in a chair in the living room watching through the large window as the sun climbed higher in the sky. As soon as she thought it was a decent enough hour, she called and left a message on Eric's business phone.

He was at her door an hour later. Wearing one of the suits he favored, he looked refreshed and handsome. His dark eyes were full of concern. "Rough night?"

Why had she never noticed before what a sexy voice he had? It seemed to get sexier each time she saw him. Or maybe it was the fact that she'd only had a few hours of broken sleep. "More like rough morning."

"You could have called my cell. You have the number."

"I know. I texted you last night, but that was a joke. I didn't want to bother you about the case outside the office."

"You're my Yoda. Master of the bad boy makeover. You're supposed to bother me."

"I made coffee. You want some?"

"Sure." He removed his jacket, and Ann admired the way his dress shirt fit. The way his lean body moved. How broad his shoulders were. She remembered how good his washboard abs had looked in his office when he'd changed his T-shirt.

"Hey? You look a little pale. Are you okay?" His hands gripped her elbows. "Why don't you sit and I'll make the coffee?"

Snapping out of it, Ann said, "No, I'm fine. I'll be right back." Fleeing into the kitchen, Ann chided herself. Thoughts of his nicely muscled chest and she was puddling at his feet? She wasn't a puddler. She didn't get breathless or giggle when it came to guys. She never had, so why now? And with Eric? "How do you take your coffee?" she called out.

"Black."

Ann returned and set the cup in front of him.

Eric opened his briefcase and removed a legal pad before patting his hand on the sofa beside him. “Sit, and let me go over some things about the case with you. Did the person who called last night give you a name?”

Ann took a seat and thought for a second. “He may have, but I don’t know that it registered with me. I was still trying to wake up.”

“Not a problem. We can get the number from Caller ID.” He made a note on the pad, then asked, “When did Lewis take over as manager?”

“January fifteenth.” The business-as-usual way Eric was speaking made Ann nervous.

“What exactly were his duties?”

“To oversee the general operations and basically handle problems as they arose.”

At that, Eric said, “Lewis couldn’t handle his way out of a paper bag. I tried to warn you.”

“You said that you didn’t like him, not that he was a sneaky, lying rat.”

“What I *said* was that he wasn’t a good fit for the company.” He reached up and loosened his tie. Though she didn’t shop at stores where an item of clothing cost enough to cover a mortgage payment, she recognized the high quality. “New tie?”

“Nancy gave it to me.”

“Nancy?” Ann wondered who the faceless woman was in Eric’s life. “Someone you care about?”

He smiled. “Very much.”

Ann didn’t know why that thought bothered her. “And she won’t mind you spending time with me?”

“Nancy is ninety-eight years old and a resident at the assisted-living facility in town. I handled a case for her. She gave me the tie because it was the last gift she’d purchased for her husband. He passed before she could give it to him."

"Oh."

"Don't worry. There's no girlfriend on the horizon at the moment. There's only you, sweetheart." He gave her an exaggerated wink, then nodded toward the legal pad. "Can we finish this?"

"Sorry." She wasn't worried about him having another woman in his life. That would be ridiculous.

"Who made the bank deposits?"

"Lewis."

"Who handled balancing the books?"

"He did." Ann cringed. "I'm good at numbers, but it was easier for him to do it so that I could concentrate on creating the chocolates, especially once I landed that deal with the New York store. Letting him handle the books, does that make me look stupid?"

"Not at all."

"Overall, though, the case doesn't paint me in the best light, does it?"

"Truthfully? No. But, people make mistakes, so don't beat yourself up about it. Besides, I've never lost a case." He tapped his arm muscle. "This brawn," then tapped the side of his forehead, "and this brain will protect you."

Ann laughed.

"You're laughing at me? Trying to give me a complex?"

"No…I just never realized what a great sense of humor you have."

"And it's amazing that I'm so good looking, too, right?"

Ann laughed again. "You're trying to make me feel better." It was working. Eric was a positive person and she admired that. Her laughter faded as she realized that she actually enjoyed his company.

"You think so, huh?" Eric redirected his attention and skimmed the notes he'd written. "Give me the last address you have for Lewis."

Ann told him, and he said, "I think that covers what I need to know for now."

As he put away the legal pad, she asked, "What happens next?"

He wouldn't look at her as he stood. "We wait."

Her intuition warned her that he wasn't telling her something. Ann rose slowly. "What's going on that you don't want me to know?"

"Ann, there's really no use in you worrying about something that's not going to happen."

"I want to know." She put her hand on his arm, then quickly moved it when he glanced down and frowned.

"I received a phone call this morning. Nothing I didn't expect. The discussion ended with the agent I was speaking with claiming criminal charges were going to be filed against you, as well as Lewis."

Ann felt like someone had punched her in the stomach. She pressed a hand against her abdomen. "Great. I'm going to end up on *America's Most Wanted*."

"Only if you run."

"Wow, that's comforting."

He grimaced. "I was making a joke but obviously not a good one. I think the agent was blowing smoke. I don't believe there will be any charges, and even if there are, they're not going to stick. There's no evidence against you of any intentional or unintentional misconduct. The only thing the government has is that it's your business. As such, they feel you did know what was going on."

"That's all it takes. I'm going down."

"All the evidence of wrongdoing points to Lewis. He's the one who deposited the money into a bank account with only his name on it. The day he left town, he cleared out that account."

"He's such a rat," Ann said.

"Definitely," Eric said with a rueful smile.

Ann's breath hitched, and her gaze dropped to his lips. He grew handsomer and sexier by the minute. She must be a lot more tired than she thought.

"I'll handle this. Try to stop worrying."

She pulled her attention away from his lips. "I think I could drain Niagara Falls easier than I could stop worrying. I was so completely blinded by him that it makes me question my own judgment. I don't think I'll be able to trust a guy again."

"Maybe you haven't spent enough time with the right kind of man."

"I'm not taking any chances. I've sworn off all of them. They've been nothing but trouble in my life. I'm going to live my life alone, surrounded by cats and knitting projects. There's not a single man I'd risk my heart on." *Especially not the one in front of me*, she reminded herself.

Eric winced and stood. "I hear you're going to the lake house after the Halloween party."

Ann thought there was a note of disappointment in his voice, but when she searched his face, he looked as calm and serious as he always did. "I am. I wasn't able to get away the last two times. Why? Are you worried we'll go fishing and I'll land the biggest one?"

Eric rolled his eyes. "My fishing skills are only superseded by my skills as a lawyer."

"Is that a challenge?" Ann asked.

"If you can dish it, I can take it." He winked.

"I can show you how to look like a sexy bad boy while we're fishing." She was playing a dangerous game, but she couldn't stop herself. Something about Eric brought out her teasing side.

He pretended to ponder. "I don't know, Ann. Alone on

the lake just the two of us, with me looking sexy, I don't know if I can take the chance you'll keep your hands to yourself. You know how your matchmaking grandfather is. Noah would FedEx a marriage license and produce a reverend before we could flee the place."

Ann grinned. "I think I can behave myself." *While tied to a chair wearing a straight jacket to keep from giving in to the urge to touch him.*

"As long as you keep that in mind." He glanced at his watch. "I've got to get to the office. Hey, if you're planning to look for a different Halloween costume, why don't we go look for one together? I still need one, and you can give me ideas."

Ann raised her eyebrows. "We can do that. I'll meet you at the party shop after you're done for the day."

As he walked out the door, he touched her arm with the tips of his fingers. "I won't let you down. I promise."

Ann nodded. She wanted so badly to believe that everything was going to work out, but she couldn't help the worry. The problem was, she was afraid she had a new worry, and it involved Eric. She didn't know what was beginning to happen, why her thoughts about him were detouring from the direction they had always taken before, but it didn't sit well with her. The more time she spent in Eric's company, the more she found things about him that she liked, admired even. Ann pulled her thoughts to a stop. It didn't matter. She wasn't about to hop on board the date-a-man train. Those tracks made stops in emotional towns like Fooled Again and Get Your Heart Broken.

She slapped her hand to her forehead. Their relationship wasn't even based on anything romantic and here she was making plans to protect herself. So silly. She rubbed the side of her temple as a headache started. But what if it could be real? What would it be like to have him kiss her and mean it? To have him hold her? She swallowed and silently chastised herself. Foolish thoughts, especially since it was Eric. But she couldn't shake how much she was looking forward to the lake house trip, because Eric was going to be there.

• • •

"You have a visitor." Eric's receptionist gave him a warning glance when he entered the office.

He walked into the waiting room and stopped in shock at the sight of his mother. Her face was pale, and her hands trembled as she clutched her purse. According to the family physician, the tremors were a chronic physical symptom of the alcoholism. He'd tried repeatedly in the past to get her to a treatment center, but she'd always refused the help. The rehab center was the last chance and that's where she should be right now rather than at his office.

"Come on in." He ushered her into his office and waited for her to speak. He couldn't imagine what this was all about. Removing her expensive coat and gloves, she eased into a seat and crossed her legs at the ankle, her back ramrod straight. Her ongoing struggle with alcoholism had ravaged the beauty Georgia Maxwell once had. To protect the family image, his father had announced she was ill whenever anyone asked why she wasn't at any of the public functions. Eric couldn't remember the last time his mother had traveled away from the family estate without his father at her side so that he could rush her away from events if he had to. "You're not well, Mom. You should be at the rehab center," he said quietly.

"I needed a break. It's nothing." She brushed off his concern as she had every time in the past.

He sighed. He'd learned years ago that you couldn't force someone to accept help if they didn't want to change. "What brings you here?"

"I know that you've taken Ann Snyder's case, and I need

you to drop it." She offered a wobbly smile. "I've spoken with your father, and we both agree that there are implications that could affect your brother's campaign."

"I'm not discussing a client's case with you."

Her lips twisted. "If she were only a client, then we wouldn't be having this conversation and you know it." Her eyes softened. "Do you think I didn't notice the difference in your tone whenever you said her name? Or how you would attend functions at the high school that you thought were boring only because you hoped for the chance to talk to her?"

"It was a long time ago."

"But the heart never forgets its first love. Eric, when the media gets wind of this, they're going to go after Ann with a vengeance. You can't get caught up in that and drag your family into it. Ann's story hitting the media is a given. Your father's already received a call from a reporter."

"Dad's not the lead agent. Why would anyone speak to him about the case?"

"I don't know but he hasn't said anything to the reporter. Yet."

Eric dropped into the chair behind his desk and stared at his mother. When he found his voice, he said, "I'm not a child anymore. His threats and emotional blackmail won't work."

She twisted her hands together. "He's only trying to protect our family."

Unable to sit still, Eric rose and walked to the window. Shoving his hands into his pockets, he stared out at the people strolling along Main Street without really registering the scene he was viewing.

"If he does talk to the media, your father could do a lot of damage to Ann and you know he has his ways. Best just to drop her as a client. We can't sacrifice your brother's political career."

Eric turned. "But you're both willing to sacrifice Ann's

future?"

She shook her head, and her lips thinned. "Eric, be reasonable. If your father doesn't slant the story, once the media gets wind of Ann's situation, they may very well start digging into our family and—"

Ah. Of course. "And the skeletons in the family closet would fall out. Wouldn't we hate that?"

Her gaze sharpened along with her tone. "Don't you judge me." His mother rose. "Will you at least consider dropping the case?"

Consider walking away from Ann when she needed him? Not a chance. He moved to open the door for her. "Not even for a second."

Her smile carried a world of sadness. "I should go."

Eric helped her put her coat on and gripped her shoulders. "I want you to get well. You shouldn't have left the rehab center."

"I had to try to talk sense into one of you." She looked away. "I'm afraid that this case will cause a war between you and your father."

What else was new? From the time he was a child, they'd been at odds. Ralph Maxwell believed in hurting whoever he had to in order to get what he wanted. They'd never see eye to eye on that.

His mother blinked back tears. "Will we see you for Thanksgiving?"

Swallowing a lump in his throat at the brokenness in her voice he said, "I wouldn't miss the latest installment of the Addams Family Thanksgiving."

Georgia smiled at that and patted his hand. "You can always handle them my way and get too blitzed to know what's going on." She started out, then paused to look back at him. "I know you'll do the right thing. You always have."

After his mother left, Eric sat and dropped his head into

his hands. Though he'd known there was a good chance Ann's story would hit the media, he'd hoped for a miracle. When a client was judged in the court of public opinion, it could be harder for the truth to be heard, and there was no doubt in his mind about the truth. Ann was innocent. She'd never take advantage of anyone.

He could go to his father, ask him to keep it off the news radar. But what would the cost be? His father wouldn't hesitate to call in favors. To offer to pay off a judge or two. He'd done it in the past. Dishonesty had never sat well with Eric, and he'd vowed he'd never be the kind of man to build a career, or a life for that matter, on dishonesty. Not to mention his father would want something from Eric in return.

But what if he did fail Ann? What if he tried his hardest and God forbid, she ended up with crushing fines to pay and a prison sentence? If she knew he'd had a chance to save her, would she end up hating him? Something told him that Ann wasn't that kind of woman, but her view might change if she was found guilty of crimes she didn't commit.

He raised his head. He'd find the answer to help Ann. As far as he was concerned, anything other than her complete exoneration wasn't an option. After he read the paperwork she'd given him for the third time, Eric saw hope. He jotted down notes and questions, not stopping until he'd filled almost three pages. A few hours later, when the phone rang, he answered it before the secretary could.

Nick called him wanting to get together and since Eric didn't have any client appointments booked for the rest of the day, he headed out. He needed to do something to occupy his mind.

He drove the 1964 Pontiac GTO he was restoring to Nick's house. Along with Chad, the three of them were going to make some adjustments to the engine and hopefully get some of the interior work finished up before the trip to the lake house.

Both men were already waiting outside when he reached the end of the winding driveway. He climbed from the car and took a second to stretch and survey the property. With several friends and family, they'd all helped Nick to put the finishing touches on the home he'd built himself. Knowing what his friend had gone through in life, Eric was glad that things were finally looking good for him.

He and Nick bumped fists and then Chad shifted forward in his chair to hand him a beer. Nodding his head, he pointed toward the car. "Good job on the primer."

"Yeah, I let Nick's cousin do that. I'm planning to get the painting done after we get back from the lake house." When he was met with silence, Eric stopped and lowered the beer, dividing his stare between the two men. His instincts told him that something was off. "What's up?"

Nick and Chad exchanged a look.

Chad reached into his back pocket and pulled out a folded paper. "A reporter called looking for information on Ann. Wanted to know if I was one of her investors. I told her no comment and hung up."

"Wasn't even an hour later that the same reporter called me," Nick said.

"Here's her number." Chad passed the paper to Eric.

Eric crumpled it into a small ball. "You'll probably be called again. Keep telling her that you don't have anything to say and warn Amelia and Abby to do the same." He regarded his friends solemnly. "It's going to get worse. What's going on with Ann is big news here, and you know how it goes."

Chad nodded. "If it's negative, it's newsworthy."

Eric popped the hood and reached beneath it to find the latch. Once he had it propped open, he said, "We're going to have to be on guard watching out for Ann. People will come out of the woodwork with claims. It'll be hard on her, seeing her family suffer, and I don't want her to carry that burden."

Nick grinned. "You've got it so bad."

Eric didn't bother to deny it. "Always have."

Chad joined him at the car. "I've known Ann all my life, and she's a great person. If it wasn't for her, I wouldn't have been able to recover from the stupid mistake I made with Amelia."

"I think I know what kind of person Ann is," Eric said. "I'm hoping that one day she'll look at me the way I look at her. Right now, I'm not even sure she likes me."

"Been there," Nick said quietly. "Like I told you before, I think you're already on your way to a tuxedo fitting. Ann wouldn't have come to you for help if she didn't like you."

Eric shrugged at that. "I was affordable."

"I don't buy that. Ann could have asked any one of us for financial help, but she didn't. I don't think that's all due to not wanting to be a burden," Chad said.

Eric thought it over. Was it possible that Ann had sought his help to feel out the possibility of there being something more between the two of them?

He walked to the rear and opened the trunk, then dismissed the thought. Maybe by the time he looked and acted like the kind of guy she normally went for, she might be interested, but he didn't think that was a possibility right now.

When they were elbow deep in parts, Abby and Noah came outside and approached Nick. Abby leaned closer to tell Nick that she was leaving for the diner and would meet him at the Halloween party.

Noah wiggled his eyebrows up and down. "Eric, Ann is lending a hand at the diner. In case you want to stop by."

"I might have some pie there in a little while."

Abby hesitated. "Is everything okay with her case? Have you heard anything?"

Eric sighed and told her the same thing he'd said to his

mother. "You know I can't discuss a client's case even if she is your sister."

"Not even a hint?"

"No."

Noah wrapped an arm around Abby's shoulders. "Attorney-client privilege. We'll ask Ann instead. She'll spill."

"How's the makeover coming? Are you seeing her tonight?" Abby asked.

"Fine, and yes. We're going to shop for our costumes."

Looking pleased at his answer, Abby waved good-bye and left with Noah.

When the car had disappeared down the driveway, Nick turned back to him. "Ah. I heard about that. The bad boy transformation." He blew him a kiss and fluttered his eyes.

"What do you want a makeover for?" Chad asked with a grin.

"Knock if off. It's a positive change, that's all." Eric's ears burned. He should have known that wouldn't stay quiet. "Originally, I came up with the idea as a way to get Ann to think of me as someone she'd date."

Nick frowned. "She has a track record of dating some real losers. I'd think you'd want to be yourself, not pattern yourself after those guys."

"I know that. There are things that could derail my hope for Ann and me. Could make everything fall apart. I have a lot of moments when I don't think there's any way Ann and I will end up dating." Eric tossed aside the rag he'd held.

"Why do you say that?" Chad asked.

"It's complicated."

"Women always are," Nick said, and Chad added his agreement.

Eric glanced at his friends, then shared what his mother had told him.

"You have to tell Ann," Nick insisted. "Warn her if you

think your father is going to talk to that reporter."

"I can't yet. I want to see how deep my father is in Ann's case first. I may be able to head him off, and then it'll never hit the news."

"That makes sense," Chad said.

"I agree, but he still needs to tell Ann in case he can't stop what might happen. Trust me, even when you're trying to do something nice for the woman you care about, it can come back and bite you. I learned that lesson," Nick insisted.

"She has enough to worry about right now. I'm hoping this all dies a very quiet death. I'm working on some things that might go in her favor. When I know for sure, I'll surprise her with the good news."

"And she'll see you as a hero and fall in love with you, right?" Nick shook his head.

Eric rubbed the back of his neck, not sure what to say to that.

"Tell her what's going on," Nick said.

The more they discussed it, the more Eric felt like his insides were being chewed on. Finally, he said, "I don't want to talk about Ann. If the two of you don't want to work on the car, maybe I should leave."

Understanding crossed Chad's face. He nudged Nick. "Let it go, man."

Nick shrugged. "All right. I'll get started on the interior."

After Nick climbed inside the car, Chad said, "I get it. You're afraid if you tell her, she'll blame you, and you're afraid if you don't tell her and something happens, she'll blame you. Like you're in a no-win situation."

"Yeah. I just need a little time. If I can get her to see me as someone she could be interested in, then I'd have a chance. That's all I've ever wanted."

"I can only speak from my experience, but when I laid it all on the line with Amelia, that's when our relationship changed. I wasn't a big fan of being vulnerable. But opening myself up turned out to be exactly what we both needed. Don't be afraid to risk everything."

Eric nodded. When he was left alone with his thoughts, his mind kept drifting back to Ann and all the ways she could end up hurt if his father shared details about the case with the media. Pushing away the turmoil inside of him, he tried to concentrate on what he was doing.

Despite his best effort, his mind kept drifting back to the information his mother had dumped on him and how it might affect Ann. Because Eric wasn't paying attention, his hand slipped, and the sharp edge of the screwdriver sliced deeply across the base of his fingers. Cursing, he dropped the tool, and grabbed a cloth to stop the bleeding. *Great.* The day kept getting better.

Chapter Seven

After a day spent bustling about the diner taking orders and helping in the kitchen, Ann's feet ached, but she wasn't sorry to be back working with her sister. She loved her chocolate shop, but she'd missed working with her family and seeing some of the regular patrons.

Though Eric had stopped by, she hadn't been able to do more than say a quick hello as she worked the tables. Now that the day was over, it was time to meet him to shop for the costume. On the way out to her car, she stopped and put her hands up to her face. She had a spring in her step, and it was the thought of seeing Eric that had put it there. Oh no. This was so not good. Maybe she should call him and tell him that she couldn't meet him. No, she couldn't do that to him. She was overreacting.

She kept telling herself that all the way to the costume shop, and when she saw Eric walking toward her, she knew she'd spent the last fifteen minutes lying to herself.

He held open the door of the shop for her, and she headed straight toward the goriest section she could find. That would take her mind off Eric. She picked up a creepy clown mask and twirled it around her fingers. "Yes?"

Eric touched the mask, and when his fingers brushed hers, Ann quickly let go of her end. "I don't really relish the thought of wearing a thick mask for three hours."

"Right. Good point."

Eric wandered over to another section and held up a Mario costume. "You could go as Princess Peach." He frowned. "But I don't like the idea of a mustache. That would itch after a while." They moved down the aisle together and both reached for similar costumes.

Ann laughed. "A gangster and a flapper. Perfect."

• • •

It wasn't until later that evening that she had qualms about her perfect costume thanks to her sisters. "What's wrong with me going as a flapper?" Ann studied her reflection. The red flapper dress sparkled in the light and had a festive feeling. She'd added the elbow length gloves and flapper headband and thought the costume looked great.

"Nothing is wrong with your outfit, but with Eric going as a gangster, it could be construed as a couples costume," Amelia said.

"So?"

"So…" Abby said as she walked into the room hopping on one foot while trying to get the other shoe on. "It means you and Eric could be included in the couples category."

"Again, so?" Ann shook her head. What was the big deal?

"*So* the winners share the prize and a nice big kiss for the local paper," Amelia reminded her.

Ann backed up and sat on the edge of the bed. "Oh." A kiss. With Eric. She bit her lip. What would that be like? Then she shook her head and looked up to find her sisters staring at her. "Our costumes aren't exactly unique." She shrugged. "The odds of us winning aren't that high." That settled, she went to the living room to wait for Eric since they were all traveling in separate cars. Fifteen minutes after her sisters left with their husbands, Ann was beginning to wonder what had kept Eric when there was a knock on the door.

Eric waited on the other side dressed in a black pinstripe suit with a black shirt and white tie. The brim of a black fedora was angled so that it hung low on his forehead, casting his eyes in shadow. His head slowly raised as he took in her outfit, and when he smiled, Ann couldn't help but smile back. She indicated his costume. "You look…" Her smile faded, and she stopped before she said sexy, "You look nice. Very 1920-ish."

He tipped his hat to her and held out his arm. "Shall we?"

She slid her hand into the crook of his arm and followed him outside, stopping on the porch when she saw the crimson and black Ford Model A. "You rented a car?"

"You like it?"

"It's beautiful, but you went all out for the night. Is Halloween your favorite holiday or something?"

He smiled. "My favorite is Christmas, but Halloween is definitely next on the list." He opened the door for her and waited until she was in before he closed it and went around the front of the car.

That was the moment when Ann could pinpoint where things took a turn. A turn for the better or the worse she wasn't sure, but she knew that there was something different. Heart racing, she stared down at her gloved hands. She felt restless, edgy, more alive. The light from the moon was brighter, the air crisper, the night stretching ahead, waiting like a paused breath. She exhaled and managed to smile as Eric drove to the community center where the party was being held.

The community center was decked out to look like a haunted house, and as they walked in, Eric put his hand at the small of Ann's back to guide her past the zombies waiting to frighten unsuspecting guests. But for Ann, the zombies didn't scare her nearly as much as her reaction to Eric's touch. She breathed out slowly, counting to ten. It didn't help take her mind off how electric, how right his hand felt against her. She whirled around to break the contact and pointed over her shoulder at a table laden with treats. "I think I'm going to get some punch. I'll bring some for you."

Ann fled to the safety of the table, nearly bumping into Amelia. "Is everything okay?"

Pasting on a smile to reassure her sister, Ann said, "Couldn't be better. Why do you ask?" Grabbing a plastic cup from the stack, she ladled punch into it.

"From the look on your face, I thought you were worried about Grandfather."

"Don't tell me he's flirting his way through the single women."

"No. Maybe I was seeing things." Amelia searched the room. "I could have sworn I saw him and Henry huddled together."

"He's probably on his matchmaking kick again," she said, knowing despite his promises not to interfere with her life that he was somehow doing it anyway.

"You don't sound too worried."

Ann paused with the punch halfway to her lips. "Grandfather is doing what he always does, and I'm not going to fret over it. I need a break from worrying about anything for one night. I came to have fun, and that's what I intend to do. So don't worry about watching out for what he's up to. Go have fun dancing with your husband." She poured a cup of punch for Eric and threaded her way through the crowd back to his side.

"Dance?" He held out his hand.

Ann set the punch down and let him link his fingers with

hers. The way she'd reacted to his touch was a fluke. Probably a chill from seeing the zombies. After they danced a few dances, including some slow ones, though, Ann knew she was wrong. It was easy being in his arms and dancing. They'd laughed, talked, and she'd enjoyed herself. When the time drew closer to hear the winners of the couples contest, Ann was so relaxed that she never saw the matchmaking punch coming.

"The winner of the couples costume contest is Eric Maxwell and Ann Snyder," the mayor announced and clapped his hands. "Come on up, you two. Claim your prize and give us a kiss for the paper."

The floor had become a pool of glue that refused to yield, and Ann slowly swung her gaze to her grandfather, who didn't even have the grace to look ashamed. He'd stuffed the ballot box. She just knew it.

"Ann?"

She lifted her head to look at Eric who didn't appear to be any happier about the turn of events than she was. Of course he wasn't. Hadn't he made it clear that she wasn't the kind of woman he was yearning to kiss? "Um…" She faked a smile, hoping no one could read the horror in her eyes.

Eric's jawline looked like it was cut of stone when he offered her his arm and led the two of them up to the front of the building. The mayor handed them each a check and then put his hands on their shoulders. "Everyone, give another round of applause to the winners." He winked at Eric. "Take it from here."

Ann recognized the reluctance on Eric's face and wished the floor would open up and swallow her whole. Her face burned, and she prayed she'd be able to keep it together enough to make it outside after…after the kiss. Her gaze dropped to his lips.

He stepped closer, sliding the palm of his hand around her waist and the silky material of her dress whispered against her skin. Her heart pounded so hard she could hear the blood rushing in her ears.

Eric's throat worked as he swallowed, and he cupped her face, gently tracing his thumb across her skin. Ann knew then she hadn't overreacted earlier. His touch did things to her. Awakened a response that made her want to move against him so that there was no space between them. The crowd of people and the complete silence in the room disappeared. Her sense of humor, her quick comebacks failed her. She parted her lips, waiting, scarcely able to breathe when he lowered his head.

Inches from her lips, Eric whispered, "I can't do this." He glanced at the photographer waiting to take their picture and raised his head, stepping back. With a smile, he addressed the crowd. "And fade to black."

People laughed and called out suggestions. Ann kept the smile frozen in place, knowing that if she didn't leave immediately, that smile was going to dissolve faster than Frosty the Snowman in the summer. Humiliated by Eric Maxwell again. Waving at the crowd, she stopped to talk to a few people she knew and even cracked a joke or two, but she didn't remember a word she'd said.

She couldn't breathe until she was outside, and then she sucked in air like she'd barely escaped drowning. Leaning back against the building, she blinked hard, stiffening when the door opened and Eric walked over to her.

"About that—"

"Oh, I know. You don't have to tell me. How awkward." She shuddered, then faked a yawn. "I have a ton of stuff to do tomorrow and more bad boy lessons to prepare, so I'd better get home and get some sleep."

He stuck his hands in his pockets and scrutinized her face like he was searching for something. She gave him a bright smile. "I'll say good-bye to everyone and meet you at the car."

It was better to walk away than to risk letting him see that she was disappointed the kiss hadn't happened. If he knew that, it could open her up to heartache or ridicule. How awkward would it be to hear him say that he wasn't interested in her "in that way?"

• • •

Eric watched her walk away. What was he missing? They'd had fun, and then her attitude had completely changed. It had to be the kiss they'd almost been forced into. Eric was thankful that he hadn't followed through even though he'd wanted it more than he'd wanted anything at that moment. But having their picture in the paper locked in a heated embrace could bring unwanted public scrutiny and might even blow back on Ann's case. He hadn't wanted that. Hadn't wanted their first kiss to be in front of the whole town, either.

The drive to her house was an exercise in frustration. Though Ann talked and responded to his questions, he could feel the distance as if she was present in body only. The second he stopped the car, she flung the door open and scurried up to her front door. Eric jumped out to follow her. "Ann, wait. What's going on?"

She shoved the key into the lock with a surprising amount of force. "Going on?"

"One minute we're having fun and the next you're freezing me out."

Her smile was phony. "I'm tired, that's all."

Sure. And I'm Superman. "If something's bothering you, maybe it would help to talk about it."

"I don't think so. Good night." At that, she shut the door in his face.

Eric rubbed the back of his neck and loosened his tie. He started to walk away, because he was pretty sure that's what a bad boy would do in her opinion. Turning around, he rang the doorbell. When she opened it, he said, "You're upset, and it has something to do with me. I don't know what it is, and you won't tell me. But I'm pretty good at puzzles, so let's play. You're upset with me because I didn't bring you flowers."

She rolled her eyes. "This isn't prom, and it wasn't a date, so no."

"You didn't deny that it was me you're upset with so I did or said something." He rubbed his chin, then sighed and tried again. "Is it because I was going to kiss you? I know that was a mistake and—"

"I'm going to bed." She shut the door and turned off the porch light.

Groaning, Eric walked down the steps and to the car. This called for reinforcements. He could call Nick and Chad, have them meet him for drinks and ask their advice on how to proceed with Ann. He stopped when he heard the steady click of a camera, and when he turned, his heart sank. A news van was parked behind the car he'd rented. He sprinted back to Ann's house and pounded on the door. When she opened it, she gasped as he maneuvered his way in and closed the door behind him. He leaned against it. "I'm sorry. I'd hoped to prevent the media from doing this."

Taking her by the hand, he shut off the living room light and pulled her to the back of the house and into the kitchen. "We don't have to worry about them taking pictures through the window in here." He exhaled, then dug out his cell phone. "I have a friend at the police department. I'll get him to run the reporters off your property, but he won't be able to keep them off the street since it's public property."

"What does all this mean?"

"It means that your story is probably going to be everywhere tomorrow. It means that they're going to show up wherever you are and hound you as well as your family for comments and information."

Ann bit her lip. "I can't let that happen."

He could tell she was trying to act strong and brave, but he could also see the fear underneath the bravado. He had to protect Ann as much as possible.

"Maybe I should give them what they want. Hold a news conference or offer to do an interview or something. Satisfy their curiosity."

"That's a bad idea at the moment."

"Then what is a good idea?"

He put a hand on her shoulder. "I live in a gated community. The media can't get in. Stay with me."

"Stay with *you*?"

"Think about it. It makes sense. You won't have reporters showing up on your doorstep, and once they realize you're not with your family, they'll leave them alone. Plus, you'll be right there if I have questions about the case, and you'll be able to work on finishing up the bad boy makeover. In fact, living together will resolve everything faster." He didn't think Ann was going to agree at first, but then she nodded.

He held up his hand. "One rule, though. No hanging your lingerie in the shower."

"I won't if you won't," she said.

Eric laughed, then sobered as he gazed down into her eyes. It was going to take every bit of strength he had to share his home with her and not end up pouring out his heart. What if this seemingly good move turned out to be the biggest mistake of his life?

Chapter Eight

No sleep and no caffeine wasn't a pleasant way to start the day. She looked over the pile of things she'd laid out to pack. Once that was done, she'd drive to Eric's condo built closer to the edge of Sweet Creek. Though she still had some misgivings about staying at his place, Eric was right. The more time she spent with him, the faster they'd be able to get the bad boy project finished, and that's what she wanted. To be done with it and the case and go back to her life.

Her normal, peaceful life where dark, soulful eyes didn't star in her dreams. So he had nice eyes. Big deal. Well, he did have a nice, muscled body. Slightly bigger deal, but she wasn't about to fork over her heart on a platter and have another man stab it. They'd live together like two civilized adults and then part ways afterward. Maybe even as good friends who could look back on their time in forced proximity with fondness. She thought about the almost kiss. *Do not go there, Ann.* All she had to do was turn Clark Kent into Superman and let him fly the coop. Let him find his Lois Lane and live happily ever after. Who cared that like Clark Kent, Eric was actually already sexy underneath those suits and glasses he sometimes wore? And without the suits?

Oh no, no, no. Don't start getting superhero ideas about Eric just because he stepped in to help. Don't forget he doesn't think you're his type. Ann slapped her forehead. She needed to think about something else. Peeking out the window, she saw the media was still camped out and that doused any of her Clark Kent fantasies. *Fantasies?* They weren't— The doorbell rang, and Ann rushed to get it, thrilled with the distraction.

Amelia walked in and gave her a hug. "I came to see if I could help."

"Thanks, Sis. I almost have the upending of my life finished." Ann looked around the cozy home she'd built for herself.

"Everything will work out. It did for Abby and for me, and look at us. We ended up married to the men of our dreams."

"Yes, but Eric is not the man of my fantasies."

Amelia frowned. "I didn't say fantasies." Her lips curled into a smile. "Something you want to share with the rest of the class?"

Ann ignored her and grabbed one of the smaller suitcases. "We rush outside and dive into the car. They'll be on us in about ten seconds, so we have to be precise." She didn't relish the thought of running through the gauntlet of reporters. "If I could get my hands on Lewis…"

"Don't give up yet. The private investigator might locate him."

Halfway into the living room, Ann paused. "I don't have the money to pay for a private investigator."

"Eric did."

"Great. I hate the thought of owing him more."

Amelia gripped the suitcase and stared at the door. "You know, announcing that you were going to move in with Eric sent Grandfather into a wedding frenzy."

"No doubt, but since there isn't a bride or a groom, there's not a lot he can do." Ann grabbed the doorknob. "Ready?" When Amelia nodded, the two of them rushed down the steps and out to Amelia's car, managing to throw the cases into the back and get in without having a single microphone shoved into their faces.

"Chad and Nick are over at Eric's clearing the guest room of all the exercise equipment."

"That explains those abs," Ann muttered.

"Abby said you'd start to see the Superman Eric is."

"One who doesn't think I'm pretty enough." Ann shook her head when Amelia demanded to know what she was talking about. The last thing she needed was for her sister to confront Eric and have him apologize and pretend that it wasn't true. She'd seen the expression of regret on his face when he'd started to kiss her at the Halloween party.

An hour later, after she'd said good-bye to her sister, Ann was officially alone in the condo with Eric. When he closed the door and turned to face her, she noticed the five o'clock shadow on his face. The concern in his eyes, the way his lips moved when he spoke. Was speaking. She blinked. "Sorry, I missed that."

"I asked if you wanted something to drink."

"Yes. Great. Perfect."

"What would you like?"

For you to take me into your arms. To feel your lips on mine. To— "You don't have to wait on me." She rushed forward toward the kitchen at the same time that he did and slammed against a torso that felt as hard as steel. She backed off and looked around his living room. "So sorry." She'd never felt such overwhelming desire to kiss a man the way she did Eric right now. Taking another step back, she bumped into an end table and spun around to catch the lamp before it hit the floor.

He held up his hands. "Ann, sit down."

She sat on the sofa and put her hands in her lap.

He disappeared for a few minutes and returned with a glass of water, crouching near her knee. "I know your life has been turned upside down, but I'll turn it right side up again." He smiled. "Okay?"

She gulped the water and set the empty glass on the table. "Okay."

"Let's go into the bedroom."

She jumped up. "I knew it! You wanted me here to... Oh...you mean the bedroom I'm going to stay in."

"You thought I was putting the moves on you?"

"No. Yes. Stupid of me. So ridiculous. I mean that...you and me...there." She pinched her lips together and gave a boisterous laugh. "Never gonna happen."

"Right." He picked up her suitcases. "This way."

She walked into the room and stopped to take it in. "Wow. It's really nice."

Eric entered behind her. "My mom went on a decorating kick before she got sick."

The warmth of his breath moved across the side of her ear, sending sparks down the side of Ann's neck. Sparks she was determined to stamp out. She would not drool over a man who didn't want her. Turning to face him, she said, "Um... your mom is sick?"

He ducked his head, but Ann didn't missed the flash of pain there. "Yeah. Listen, why don't we have an early lunch?"

Ann followed him back into the living room. "We can do that with the media after me?"

Eric pressed a security panel and brought up a small screen. "They're not at the gate. See? Plus, we can eat somewhere outside of Sweet Creek."

"And afterward, I'll help you pick out some clothes, and you can help me take care of the rest of my truffles."

"As in eating them for dessert?"

"Works for me." She laughed and tried desperately not to think about Eric and chocolate.

• • •

Eric had to admit that even though Ann was acting a little strange, he couldn't remember the last time he'd had as much fun. Despite all her troubles, Ann never let the negativity of the situation make her feel sorry for herself. He admired that.

The journey to the chocolate shop didn't take long, but the streetlights were already beginning to flicker on as he parked. Ann unlocked the shop and stepped in. Eric closed the door behind them, and instantly they were surrounded by silence. Though she wasn't showing it, being in the shop, seeing it this way, had to hurt, and that made his heart ache.

She set her purse down on the counter. "There are probably enough chocolates for several dozen bags. We can each take one, and I'll give the others away. I can take some to the diner and some to—" Her voice ended on a broken note.

Unable to stop himself, Eric walked up behind her and put his hands on her shoulders. "I swear that I'll fight with every breath I have to make this right for you." He was going to offer her comfort with his words and nothing more, but his game plan changed when she turned around in his arms. The tears tracking down her face were his undoing.

"Ann." His voice was barely above a whisper. He tightened his grip, not pulling her to him or pushing her away, leaving the next move up to her. His heart beat faster and his mouth went dry when she leaned into him, letting her head come to rest against his chest.

Raising his hand, he rested it on the back of her hair, gently stroking. She shifted her arms and slowly wrapped them around his waist. Wanting her, but not able to have her was the sweetest agony, but he knew better than to make a move.

She lifted her head and leaned back so that she could look into his eyes. "Kiss me."

His eyes widened. "Do you realize what you just asked me?"

"Yes." She lowered her gaze, and a hesitant smile crossed her lips. "I didn't think… I mean, if you don't want to, that's fine."

Sliding his fingers beneath her chin, he tilted her face up to his. "I have never wanted anything more than to kiss you."

She looked surprised by that. "But?"

"Here in the shop, the emotions and thoughts have to be running rampant through you right now. I don't want to be your caught-in-the-moment mistake." He smoothed her hair away from her eyes. "Ask me again when your heart isn't overwhelmed."

Ann pulled away, a flush creeping up her face. "What makes you think I'll ask again?"

His heart skipped. "Because you're my Lois Lane. You won't be able to help yourself."

His teasing had the desired effect, and Ann laughed, rolling her eyes. Putting some space between them, she asked, "So which truffles are your favorite?"

"All of them."

She laughed again and walked around the counter to snap open a bag. "Then fill it up."

As he started choosing the chocolates, she said, "Be right back. I think I have some drinks left in the refrigerator." She headed to the kitchen and was back in seconds with two bottles of chilled coffee. "I have French vanilla and French vanilla. Which one would you like?"

He pretended to think about it. "I'm going to go out on a limb and choose French vanilla." She passed him a bottle, and their hands brushed. He didn't imagine the slight inhale she took, and the action filled him with hope. Was it possible that she was genuinely attracted to him, and it had nothing to do with her being besieged by emotions about the shop?

Ann twisted the cap off her drink and grabbed a couple of the truffles. She lowered herself until she sat cross-legged on the floor with her back against the wall facing the display cases.

Eric took his bag of truffles and the coffee, then joined her. He stretched his legs out and searched the bag for one of the hazelnut chocolates.

Ann set her drink down and wiped her mouth with her fingers. "Do you remember when we were in high school and you and your friends created that fantasy girl draft?"

He grimaced. "Yeah. Not our finest hour."

"I think maybe..." She darted a look at him. "That's why we weren't friends in high school. Then as the years passed, we never seemed to get along, and every time I talked to you, I always ended up feeling rattled."

"We're getting along now." He pointed out. He'd always liked how opinionated Ann was, how strong she was, but he couldn't help wondering if she used bravado to hide behind when she was hurting.

"Only because I need a lawyer and you wanted help becoming less of a nerd. Otherwise, we wouldn't be here."

"Don't be so sure about that. Fate has a way of working things out regardless of our intentions."

She took a sip of her drink. "You and I could never work because you have such awful taste in music."

He studied her, then took her hand in his and held it to his heart. "I could go to music therapy."

Ann smiled and nudged him with her elbow before she pulled away. "There's not enough therapy in the world for you."

"No?"

"No." She glanced at him, then grabbed a napkin. "You have a smudge of chocolate." Leaning closer, she rose to her knees and wiped the corner of his mouth.

Eric froze for a second, then lifted his hand to capture hers. He intended to lower her hand, diffuse the tension rising in his body, but that was before her lips parted ever so slightly. Before her eyes darkened. Before she whispered, "My heart's not feeling overwhelmed right now."

• • •

Ann couldn't believe what she'd said. Practically begging him to kiss her. She had no excuse other than she wanted this. Maybe they'd kiss and she wouldn't experience any sizzle, or any longing. Maybe she only thought she was attracted to him but really wasn't.

She thought he was going to refuse her again.

He shifted closer, then moved swiftly, pulling her onto his lap so that she faced him. Studying her face, he grinned.

Ann lowered her head until their foreheads rested together. "What?"

"Like I said. You're my Lois Lane."

She ran her hands across the expanse of his shirt, then lifted his hand and put it against her chest. "Feel how fast my heart is beating."

"Likewise."

"Maybe our hearts are racing because we're experiencing something like an adrenaline rush."

"Could be." He traced her lips.

She pressed a kiss to his finger.

He ran his fingers through her hair, and Ann arched her neck, waiting to feel his lips against her skin. When he didn't move, she opened her eyes. "Eric?"

"You haven't asked me yet."

"Are you being difficult?"

"Are you going to ask?"

"Clark Kent, will you kiss me?"

His chest shook with laughter, and he lowered his hands to her waist before skimming them up her back and pressing her forward. When their lips met, Ann knew she was in trouble. The sizzle and the longing were definitely present. The warmth of his mouth on hers zipped through her. She parted her lips, allowing his tongue to tangle with hers. He tasted like hazelnut and coffee and delicious, body-warming, sense-numbing heat. Though she was sitting in his lap, she was still too far away. Pushing closer, she ran her hands over his arms, reveling in the strength of his body.

He deepened the kiss, making it more urgent, and Ann accepted it all, her body on fire, her mind racing along with her heart. She lowered her hands to the sides of his shirt, inching them upward. It wasn't until she felt the cooler air on her back that she realized her own button up shirt was hanging off the back of her shoulders. She pulled away and closed her eyes as his lips found the base of her neck. Somehow, she had to find the strength to stop, or she and Eric were going to end up tangled together on the floor. "Eric." If the media happened to find them here, wouldn't that give them an eyeful?

He exhaled, and his breath bathed her chest in warmth. "Give me a second," he said in a voice still thick with need.

"I don't know what this is, and it scares me," she admitted, brushing her tangled hair away from her face.

Gently reaching forward, he resettled her shirt and began fastening the buttons. "It was a kiss. Did you want it to be more?"

"No. Yes." Ann scooted off his lap and rose, facing away from him. She finger combed her hair when it flopped in front of her eyes. "I don't know." She swung around to look at him.

"Do you?" *I think I want him to say yes.*

A shutter came down across his face, and he spoke slowly as if he was being cautious, "Why don't we wait and see what tomorrow brings?"

She wasn't an idiot. He wanted her, that much was clear, so why was he so reluctant to admit it? Unless she'd misread the cues. Had he been flirting with her, or had she only seen what she'd wanted to see? No, he'd kissed her like a man who wanted her.

She pressed a finger to her temple, feeling confused. Had Eric only kissed her because she was here and she'd flirted and asked him to? It wouldn't be the first time she'd gotten her cues mixed up. She did have a bad radar where men were concerned. *Please, please don't let me make another mistake.* "Okay, we can wait and see what tomorrow brings."

Ann picked up the truffles she'd bagged up. She needed some space. "We should leave. Once we get back to your place, let's go over another lesson. I want to make sure I help you so that you don't feel cheated."

"I don't feel— Ann, hold on."

He caught up to her at the door and swung her around to face him. "I feel as if I've done something wrong."

"It's nothing."

"Come on. You've never been afraid to speak your mind before."

She made a noise and thrust the truffle bags into his arms. "If you'll take these, I'll lock up."

"You're upset."

He sounded so astonished that Ann clenched her teeth together. Then as quickly as she did so, she relaxed. If she was confused about what she wanted, she couldn't expect him to be sure of anything, either. She locked the door and took the bags back before heading toward the car. "You're right. It was a kiss, nothing more, and I overreacted."

She climbed into Eric's car and fastened the seatbelt. Her limbs were shaky as if she'd run a marathon. The kiss had held an intensity and power that rocked her and pushed at the walls she'd built to guard herself from Eric or any other guy. Physical attraction she understood, but she'd never experienced anything like this before. She stared through the windshield at Eric as he walked to the car.

She was attracted to him; she'd admit that. It shocked her how fast the attraction had slammed into her, or had it always existed and she'd been blind to it? Not that it mattered. Her life was in chaos right now. The last thing she needed to do was jump into another relationship that was sure to be doomed, especially since Eric wanted her to help him become exactly the kind of man she avoided.

Chapter Nine

"So I'm not supposed to be honest? You said 'be honest, be real,' and I was, before you even told me to be. Now you're saying that I did the wrong thing?" Eric demanded later that evening as the two of them were seated on the sofa. He leaned forward to set his beer on the coffee table.

Ann could understand his frustration. Dating was never easy. She tucked a strand of her hair behind her ear. "You don't tell a date that she's clingy."

"She asked me if I thought she was clingy. I wasn't going to lie and encourage the way she was acting. I walked to the men's room, turned around, and she was right behind me."

"Maybe she had to go to the ladies' room."

"No. She told me she'd wait outside the door for me and walk with me back to the table."

"Okay, so she was clingy. If that's the worst you've ever experienced dating, then consider yourself lucky."

Resting his head against the sofa cushion, Eric thought for a second. "No, the worst one was the woman who told me that I had to meet her friend Bob first. She said he screened all her dates."

Ann nodded. "She was being smart. There's nothing wrong with a woman being careful."

Eric lifted an eyebrow. "Bob was her cat. She wanted me to have a conversation with him. She said he would send her telepathic waves to let her know if he approved of me or not."

Laughing, Ann said, "What did you do?"

"I told her Bob said I wasn't the right guy for her and got the hell out of there." He grinned at the memory. "What about you? Worst date?"

"A few years ago, I let a friend set me up on a blind date. He took me to a tobacco-spitting contest."

"Are you serious?"

"I wish I wasn't."

"Well, that's romantic. You didn't fall in love on the spot?"

Ann reached down and eased her shoes off. "The worst part was that his mother won. After she collected her trophy, she spit a stream of tobacco juice out and told her son that I was a keeper."

Eric laughed.

"Yep. I never went on another blind date after that." She yawned and stretched. "I'm getting up early to help Abby open the diner and then there's the trip to the lake house afterward, so I'm going to head to bed. But to recap the lesson, do be honest, but tactfully so."

"Okay. So when the date asked me if she was clingy, I should have held her hand and told her yes, that she was clingy but in a cute way like one of those suction cup window animals."

"The rule doesn't apply to someone who's weird. Dates like that get interrupted with a 'sorry, I have to go' excuse."

"It seems rude to treat someone that way."

Ann lifted her shoulder in a shrug and rose. "It's not. Healthy relationships don't include clingers, telepathic cats, or tobacco-spitting potential mother-in-laws." She paused for a second. "Not that I'm an expert on dating, given my history."

Eric rose to stand beside her. "It's not your fault that the men in your life weren't what they should have been."

"I should have seen it, should have had some kind of internal warning that something was wrong."

"No."

Ann looked at him, her eyebrows raised. The vehemence in his voice surprised her.

"When a guy is a jerk or unfaithful or he's a con man, to turn around and say the woman or the other party should have known is bull. That's taking the blame and the responsibility off the person who's less than he should be and putting it on the shoulders of the person he hurt."

"You sound very passionate about that."

He put his hands in his pockets. "My final year in law school, I volunteered at a women's shelter. There was a woman there whose husband was an abusive waste of breath. They married after having dated for two years. Her family blamed her, asked her why she didn't see any signs, and how he could have fooled her for so long."

"Wow. First the husband, then the family."

"Exactly. I told her that her family was asking the wrong questions. The questions weren't what did she miss or how could he have fooled her, but why was he abusive. People who want to fool others or take advantage of people always find a way, Ann."

"Like Lewis."

"Yes," he agreed.

"Amelia said that you hired a private detective to find him."

He glanced away.

"Eric?"

"Uh...yeah, I did."

"You're putting a lot into this case, and I'm struggling to believe that you're doing it all simply because you want a makeover. Is there something else you're not saying? Do you have a deeper reason for helping me?" Her heart seemed to beat faster as she waited for his response.

"Of course not." He held her gaze for a moment, then glanced at his watch. "It's getting late, and you said that you have to be up early."

"Right, and I doubt we'd be able to solve my situation no matter how long we talked about it." Her smile faltered as she searched his face.

Eric picked up the remote for the electric fireplace and turned from her. Clicking it off, he tossed the remote back and forth in his hands for a second, then put it back on the side table. He seemed torn about something as he gave her a tight smile. "Good night, Ann." He strode away from her toward his bedroom.

Ann bit her lip. What wasn't he telling her?

• • •

Shivering, Ann hurried into the warmth of the diner. She and Abby, along with the rest of the staff, had to get things started for the breakfast regulars. Taking off her sweater, she hung it on a hook in the back of the kitchen and reached for an apron, then headed for the coffee pot.

"Hey," she greeted Abby as she poured herself a cup.

Abby slid another mug toward her. "Fill me up. I was awake most of the night."

Ann grinned, and Abby shook her head. "It's not what you think. Granddaddy was staying over, and I was up all night worrying about him. He left to run an errand and didn't return until morning. I called his cell."

"Is he okay?"

"When I finally reached him, he told me he'd gone on a date."

"A *date*?"

Abby nodded. "He refused to discuss with who and that worries me. What if he's seeing someone who's planning to take advantage of him?"

Ann laughed. "I don't think that's a problem." She opened the refrigerator and took out the cinnamon rolls she and Abby had put together the day before. After preheating the oven, she continued, "Granddaddy has a sharp mind. He'll run mental circles around anyone who even tries to get one over on him."

"I guess you're right, but why wouldn't he tell me?"

"Maybe he didn't think you'd approve."

"That's silly. I want him to be happy. He knows that."

"Then let him have his little intrigue. Besides, it keeps him from meddling in my life." Ann grinned.

Abby put on an apron and slid the rolls into the oven. "I guess so. How's that going with Eric and the case?"

"No movement on the case."

"I sensed a hesitation." Abby rinsed her hands and took a bowl of eggs from the refrigerator.

"It's not something that I can put my finger on. An intuition that something's going on that I'm not going to like."

"With Eric, or with your case? How's it going living with the enemy?"

"He's not so much the enemy anymore." Measuring out flour for the pancakes, Ann dumped it in a bowl, then stirred in eggs and a dash of cinnamon before she answered. "You were right. Eric's a good guy, and he's fun."

"Not to mention handsome."

Ann turned the griddle on. "Yes, he is." Whisking the batter, she said, "What I don't understand is why he wanted this bad boy makeover. He seems to like who he is. I don't get the sense that he plays head games, so what's his agenda?"

"Maybe he doesn't have an agenda. It could be that he genuinely wanted to change his life."

"Why now? I mean, didn't he want to make changes before I needed his help?"

"Who knows? It could have simply been a situation where he wanted help but didn't think of anyone he could turn to until you came along."

"Maybe." Ann poured a round circle of batter onto the griddle. "Is Amelia coming in?"

"After lunch. Morning sickness has been a struggle for her."

A light knock sounded on the back door, and Ann jumped, glancing at the clock. "It's not even six thirty yet. Who could that be?"

Abby went to the door and cautiously peeked out. "It's Eric." She let him in.

"Ann left her wallet. I thought she might need it."

Ann passed the spatula to her sister. "I can't believe I drove over here without my license. I cleaned out my purse and I guess I forgot to put my wallet back in. Thanks." She took it from him. "You didn't fix your tie."

"I left the condo in a hurry. I have a meeting at seven thirty at the marina."

From the expression on his face, she could tell he wasn't looking forward to that, but she didn't want to pry. "You want to take some coffee with you?"

"That'd be great." He waited while she searched for a to-go cup.

"You're meeting a client at the marina?" Ann secured a lid on the cup and passed it to him. She moved closer. *Why does he have to smell so amazing?* "Hold still." Grasping the ends of his tie, she quickly tied it in a half-Windsor, then smoothed the material flat against his dress shirt.

"Thanks."

Ann lowered her hands, realizing that he hadn't answered about whether or not he was meeting a client. It wasn't any of her business who he was going to see. "Good luck with your meeting."

He nodded and winced before muttering, "I'm going to need it."

Abby called over to them, "I'm making some sandwiches to take to the lake house this afternoon. Any preferences?"

"I'll eat anything." Eric backed toward the door. "See you later."

After he left, Abby said, "The thing with the tie? You sure looked comfortable doing that."

"It's easy being around Eric."

"Oh. So, there are no sparks?"

Ann considered denying it, then decided to tell the truth. "There are sparks, and he kisses in a way that makes me feel breathless and fizzy inside."

"Kisses, huh?" Abby grinned. "You like him."

"I do like him." Ann grinned back, but then her smile faded. "What if he turns out to be no better than my ex-fiancé?"

Abby hurried to the grill and slid a pancake onto a plate. "Do you honestly think that Eric is like that?"

"No, I don't, I guess."

"You're afraid, and I don't blame you after what you've been through, but if you let fear dictate your actions, then you never move forward, never reach healing. I speak from experience, don't forget."

"I know, but it's a little different with me." Ann gathered a stack of menus. "If you check back over my dating history, every single guy I've dated has turned out to be a dud. So either men suck or I suck at picking them, in which case I'm better off alone."

"Don't close yourself off, Ann. I spent too many wasted years like that."

Ann checked the clock. "I'm fine. I'll go unlock the front door. Did you make enough pancakes for Oscar and Sue?"

"Yep. They always order the same thing every morning."

Ann walked into the dining room area and put the menus by the cash register, then switched the closed sign to open before unlocking the front door. Oscar and Sue were already heading up the sidewalk, hand in hand. Ann gave them a wave through the glass and went back to help Abby, thinking about what her sister had said. Was she truly ready to move forward? Why did an image of Eric pop into her mind when she asked that question?

• • •

Eric didn't waste any time on small talk once the private investigator docked. "You said you had something. What is it?"

The older man pulled out a folder. "Surveillance photos. He never left the country. He's been staying on a houseboat. The one that's docked a few slips over. I included the information on the owner of that boat. You gonna grab him?"

"I can't do anything yet. He hasn't been formally charged with a crime."

"Well, you might not want to let too much grass grow under your feet before you do something. I followed the guy to a bar last night. He had a meeting." The investigator tapped the folder. "Those pictures are in there, too."

Eric opened the folder and flipped through the photos. One in particular troubled him. The woman in the photo with Lewis looked familiar, but he couldn't quite figure out why. "Stay on him, and if he makes any move like he's even considering leaving the area, call me."

Eric headed back to his car. He needed something, anything to get Lewis, especially after learning that a grand jury was deciding whether or not to formally indict Ann. He'd never thought it would get this far. He didn't know how he was going to break the news to her. Having a grand jury convene wasn't good, and he'd been around the law long enough to know many prosecutors were in favor of them since the jury would see what the prosecutor wanted them to see. He wouldn't have the chance to defend Ann before the grand jury.

After he reached his office, Eric took out his cell phone. He could talk to his father, have him call in a few favors and make Ann's case go away. He hit the button for the speed dial for his father's number. But if he asked for this, it would get easier to step farther over the line of what was right and what was wrong, like his father. Easier to manipulate and dictate. Easier to look into the mirror and not recognize the man staring back. Not to mention his father would hold it over him. Who knew what he'd ask Eric to do as repayment for the favor. He squeezed the phone hard, then put it away and reached for the phone on his desk to dial the prosecutor's office.

Chapter Ten

Right before lunch, Abby asked Ann to make a supply run. Ann whipped off her apron and grabbed her sweater, glad to take a break. Though the diner had kept her busy, she hadn't been able to take her mind off Eric or the kiss they'd shared. Maybe getting out into the fresh air would clear her thoughts.

"I'll be back as soon as I can."

Abby waved her hand. "Take your time. Since we're heading to the lake, I arranged for all my waitresses to come in for the afternoon, so the diner's under control."

Ann went out to her car, going over her mental to-do list. Her stomach growled. She should have thought to get some lunch sooner. She glanced at the clock. There was enough time for her to whip into Smashburger and grab a hamburger before she picked up the supplies. She parked in the last remaining spot at the restaurant and stepped out, heading to the front entrance. As she stepped onto the sidewalk and skirted one of the black iron table and chair sets, she froze.

Walking toward her, arm in arm was Monica and Ann's ex-fiancé. They both gave her tentative smiles. "Um…you should probably hear this from us." Monica held out her left hand where a diamond engagement ring sparkled. "We're getting married."

Ann didn't bother to look at it. She directed her smile at her ex. "I just realized the irony of your initials, Steven Thomas Deering." Excusing herself, Ann walked into the restaurant and rested with her back against a wall. She waited until Monica and her ex moved out of sight down the sidewalk before she went back to her car. There was no way that she could eat lunch now with her stomach in such turmoil. Digging out her cell phone, she meant to dial her granddaddy but accidentally called Eric instead.

He answered on the first ring.

She took a deep breath. "Sorry. I hit the wrong button."

"Is everything okay?"

"If you call running into your ex and his new fiancée, Monica Sinclair, okay."

"That's a tough one. I've been there."

Ann frowned. "You were engaged?"

"No. I ran into your ex and Monica. You know his initials are STD, right?"

Ann laughed and gripped the phone. "I told him that."

Eric laughed with her. "Do you need me? If you want to talk, I can meet you somewhere."

"No, I think I'm okay. It was a shock, that's all. He and Monica deserve each other."

"I agree. If you change your mind about needing to talk, call me."

"Where are you?"

"I'm at the barbershop. I asked for a bad boy haircut, and I think he's giving me a Mohawk."

Ann laughed again. "You *are* joking, right?"

"What do you think?"

"I think you should get a piercing," she teased.

"I will if you will."

She smiled. "I better go before Abby wonders where I am."

"Okay. I'll meet you later. Make sure you bring your sexiest bikini for the lake trip."

"I skinny dip." She hung up on his sputtered laugh and still smiling, drove toward the supply store. Her smile fell when she realized that talking to Eric was what had made her feel better again.

• • •

Later that afternoon, Eric closed up the office early to go home and pack for the trip to the lake. He'd made several phone calls on Ann's behalf and was waiting for return calls. With it being the weekend, he hadn't had much luck reaching the people he needed to talk to. Like him, they'd probably cut out of work early.

He'd figured out that the person in the photo with Lewis was a socialite his mother knew. No doubt Lewis was working a scam on her. He'd contact the woman and hopefully get her help getting to Lewis. He was a con man, but he wasn't the brightest bulb in the pack.

He walked into the condo, and even though she wasn't there, the scent of Ann's perfume curled around him like a caress. He'd thought about her throughout the night and all morning long. He was tired of not acting on his feelings. If everything went according to plan, they'd have this weekend together, and then, he'd find a quiet place alone with her and tell her that he was crazy in love with her.

After packing a bag with clothes and toiletries, he locked up and climbed into the Pontiac GTO to drive to Noah's house where everyone had agreed to meet.

The tension from the week started rolling off. The idea of

a weekend at the lake house had that effect. He could escape the rat race and simply chill. He wished that he could lie to himself that the fact he would get to spend more time with Ann had nothing to do with his excitement. Had nothing to do with her being kind, funny, and sexy. But he wasn't that good at lying.

Hell, maybe he was so caught up in wanting her because of how he'd felt about her in high school. He'd wanted to be the hero to rescue her from all her hurts once he'd found out what happened to her parents and later with her cheating fiancé.

Sighing, he turned the heater off. The fall day was caught between a temperature that was too warm for heat but too cool for the air.

Reaching the house, he parked behind the twelve-passenger van they'd all chipped in to rent. Growing up, whenever he and his siblings had to travel out of town, it was always by limousine or private plane. Quiet, staid trips that had bored him nearly out of his mind. With Ann's family, things were never boring.

As soon as he had his gear stowed in the back, Ann pulled her car up in front of the house and climbed out. He wished he didn't notice how good she looked in jeans that showed off her curves. Or how her hair fell in waves around her face. Or how her lips were coated with a soft pink color that begged for a kiss. But he'd always noticed her, would always notice her.

"Hi." She handed him her bag. "Your haircut looks great. Very sexy."

Eric paused. "Are you being sarcastic?"

She looked surprised. "Not at all." She checked out the van. "Why such a big van? There are only six of us going."

The front door of her grandfather's house flung open, and Noah shuffled down the walk with a bag. He was followed by his best friend, Henry Walker, Chad's grandfather.

Eric shrugged when Ann raised her eyebrows. Crossing her arms, she called out to her grandfather, "Please tell me that you're not going just to play matchmaker."

"Of course not. Wouldn't think of it." Noah helped Henry store his bag. Henry had been diagnosed with a terminal heart condition shortly before Chad and Amelia had married. His health was one of the reasons he and Noah had tricked Amelia and Chad into marrying with their meddling.

Eric swung open the passenger side door. "The more the merrier."

Amelia climbed in first, with Chad making sure she didn't trip. "I haven't taken a group road trip since college. This should be fun."

Ever since Amelia had announced her pregnancy, Chad had hovered. Not that Eric blamed his friend. It was easy to see how much the once die-hard anti-love guy loved his wife.

After some discussion, it was decided that Eric would drive the three hours to the lake house. He got behind the wheel and motioned for Ann to take the front passenger seat. He started the van. "Hope you brought your best game for the fishing."

"Oh, please. My best game goes everywhere that I go." She tugged the seatbelt and fastened it around herself. "I've been thinking about something to do with the case."

Eric shook his head. "We both need to relax. No discussing the case until after the trip is over." At first, he thought she'd object, but Ann nodded.

"I brought some homemade snacks," Amelia volunteered. There was silence until she sighed and added, "I wasn't the one to make them." She dug out a container full of M&M brownies and passed them around. Snapping the lid shut, she muttered, "Add a half cup of salt just once and everyone freaks out."

Laughter filled the van as Eric backed out and headed for the interstate.

The trip went smoothly, but they hit their first snag after they'd arrived, when they were dividing up the bedrooms.

Ann looked around at her family. "What do you mean I have to share the room with Eric? We're not a couple, and you all know that."

"I know, but the rooms are already claimed by the rest of us. The first to call it gets the rights," Nick said. "Rules are rules."

Turning to face her sisters, knowing they'd help her out, Ann said, "Then I guess the guys can double up, and I'll share a room with one of you."

No happy campers greeted her suggestion. *Seriously*?

"I really wanted to spend the time with Nick," Abby said. She bumped her husband's shoulder playfully. "We've been so busy lately we haven't had any—"

Ann made a gagging motion and held her hand up. "I don't need a blueprint." She looked at Amelia with raised eyebrows.

"Same here, Ann."

Ann put her hands on her hips. Surely she'd find mercy with her youngest sister. "You're already pregnant, Ame. Don't you need your sleep?"

"Sorry, Sis, but I'm not bunking with you," Amelia said.

"Granddaddy?"

"No can do, honey. Henry and I have plans to stay up late and sleep in. Our hours wouldn't be compatible." He tried to look innocent but failed.

Ann looked at Eric. "Did you arrange this so that we'd have to spend the night in the same room?"

"Me? I thought it was your idea." He picked up his bag. "Look, if you're worried that you'll jump me in the middle of the night, I'll sleep on the floor of the living room."

"Jump you? Why would I jump you?"

"Oh, I don't know. Maybe it's because you nearly stripped me naked when you kissed me?"

"You weren't even close to naked." The color rose in her cheeks, and Ann snapped, "And *you* kissed me!"

"But you asked me to," he pointed out.

Abby looked back and forth between them, then asked, "Are you two dating?"

"No!" Ann said, then snatched up her bag and marched toward the bedroom.

"You should be so lucky," Eric called to her.

"*Lucky*?" She wasn't sure if she was upset at the idea that Eric might have maneuvered the situation to get her alone with him or the fact that she *did* want to be alone with him.

"I get the top bunk," she said as soon as Eric joined her in the room. After taking a deep breath and exhaling to calm herself, she said, "I'm sorry. This isn't your fault. I don't really believe that you'd try to manipulate me into bed with you."

"Of course I wouldn't. If anything, I'd be fighting you off."

Oh, really. She traced her fingers over the design on the bedspread. "Would you?"

• • •

Eric stilled and the humor drained from his face. "Would I what?" He didn't want her asking him questions like that. Not if she wasn't serious.

She shook her head. "Never mind. I'm not really upset about the sleeping arrangements." She sighed and glanced at him. "I don't have any romantic feelings whatsoever for my lousy ex-fiancé, but seeing him today was like a slap in the face. It reminded me how I felt when I caught him cheating. So humiliated and shocked."

The burn started in Eric's stomach. He hated that she'd

had that experience, and it made it understandable why she was so cautious around him. "I'm sorry."

Ann shrugged. "I lived."

"Please tell me he wasn't one of the bad boys in your life."

"He was actually, but I don't really like that type of guy." Her eyes widened. "Not that I don't like you. Or think you're being foolish for wanting a change. I just…um…that's not the kind of guy for me."

This was it. He was going to tell her why he'd wanted the stupid makeover in the first place. "Ann—"

Noah poked his head into the room. "Happy birthday, Eric."

Eric spun around, not sure if he was upset or glad at the intrusion. "It's not my birthday."

"No kidding. Come help us unload the van."

Ann laughed and explained, "The only days we were excused from any kind of work when I was growing up was on our birthdays. If we weren't helping out, Granddaddy would always ask if it was our birthday."

"Ah." Eric left the room and quickly walked beside Noah back to the van.

"Is it my imagination or were you about to kiss Ann?"

"It's your imagination." *Liar.*

"Comes with getting older," Noah said.

The older man smiled in a serene way that caused a warning to start in Eric's gut. He was willing to bet Noah was up to something and that it involved pushing him and Ann together. He'd take care of that right now. He wanted Ann on her own terms and not because she was pressured. "Ann is my client."

"Yep, I know that."

"I'm her attorney."

Noah gave him a side-eye glance. "I'm old but not so old that I couldn't figure that out, too."

"I meant that's all I am."

"Do you kiss all your clients?"

"What? No."

"Just some of them?"

Eric sighed. "Noah… I have to keep my focus on helping Ann. There are things going on that you don't know and that I can't talk to you about. So case closed."

"Case needs to be retried if you ask me."

"I didn't ask."

"Well, that's one of the benefits of getting older. Us old folks can get nosy and give our two cents, even where it doesn't belong. Ann might act like she's tough and not interested, but her heart has been waiting for the right man to come along."

"I suppose that you think I'm the man for her." Eric glanced back toward the house.

Noah clasped his hand on his shoulder. "The real question is do you believe you're the man for her?"

Eric took a breath. "I want you to back off."

Noah's eyebrows winged upward. "You've always been crazy about Ann. What's going on?"

"Nothing I can't handle."

Noah scratched his head. "If you like my granddaughter, and there's no reason why you shouldn't, then you need to tell her so."

"You've always thought Ann and I would make a great couple."

Picking up a bag with some food supplies, Noah swung it out of the van and said, "Right and that's what I told your mother." Noah's face instantly paled. He tried to head back into the house, but Eric stepped in front of him with his hand raised in a stop gesture.

"Hold on. How do you even know my mother?"

Noah's gaze shifted toward the house as if he was looking for a way out of the conversation. When Eric wouldn't move,

Noah finally said, "We met when your mother was making her big break from the rehab center. She ran right out in front of my car, and I stopped to help her. Gave her a ride to your office. After she learned who I was and what I thought of you and Ann together, I thought she was going to help. Then I heard she tried to talk you out of taking Ann's case."

Eric clenched his jaw. "Is that all the meddling you've done?"

Noah made a crossing motion over his chest. "I swear."

"You know I don't believe you're innocent in anything that you do."

"That's because you've been around too many guilty people." He offered up a smile, then said, "So, what's on your agenda tomorrow morning?"

"I'm going fishing with Ann."

"She always brought home the trophy for the biggest catch from summer camp every year that she went. Hope you're not challenging her." Whistling, Noah headed back to the house, and Eric couldn't shake the feeling that when Noah said challenging, he wasn't talking about fishing.

• • •

When her grandfather returned to the house, followed by Eric, Ann raised her eyebrows. Eric simply shook his head, and she knew that Noah had been up to something. Well, let him meddle. She was on to him and knowing how he'd operated with her sisters, she'd be able to keep him in line and sidestep him trying to maneuver her and Eric together.

"I think Granddaddy's up to something," she said. Taking the lettuce and tomatoes out of the bag, she walked over to the sink and started washing them.

Abby worked on creating the sauce to pour over the steaks and then gave the platter to Nick to take outside to the grill. "When is he not?"

"I don't think he sees it as meddling. I think that Granddaddy is feeling the pressure," Amelia said quietly.

"Pressure from what?" Chad walked into the kitchen and rolled up his sleeves.

"From the passing of time. I think that he is genuinely worried about what will happen to us once he's gone. He's trying in his own way to look out for us."

The sisters shared a pained look at the thought of Noah not being with them.

"That's why it's so hard to get upset with him," Ann said. She tore the lettuce up into pieces and then set to work chopping the tomatoes. "But if he had his way, Eric and I would be together, regardless of the way that Eric feels about that."

"And you, too?" Abby asked with a question in her eyes.

One that Ann hastened to answer. "I don't know. But if things continue to go south for me, Granddaddy won't have to worry about my future. I'll be taken care of for between five and ten years, courtesy of the state."

"Sounds like you need something to take your mind off your worries," Abby said. "I have an idea."

"Thanks, Sis, but I don't think looking at pictures of hot guys is going to help."

Ann laughed along with Amelia. Abby swatted them both with a kitchen towel. "Seriously, we should watch a scary movie tonight."

Ann shivered. Trying to sit through a horror movie would definitely take her mind off her troubles, but she'd prefer not to see one when they were in the middle of the woods. "Too spooky. Besides, I'm not really in a movie mood."

"Get out here, woman. The food is ready," Nick called into the kitchen.

Abby raised her eyebrows at her husband. "Maybe I do

need to share a room with my sister."

Nick was in the kitchen instantly, coming up behind Abby, wrapping his arms around her. He kissed the side of her neck. "Consider this my deepest apology."

Ann laughed along with the others, but that pang of hurt she'd experienced once again, this time over what Lewis had done, rose up to remind her to be careful. She wanted what her sisters had, but she didn't want to risk the heartache that went along with it. What if Abby had fallen for Nick and it hadn't worked out? Or what if Chad and Amelia hadn't? They were both strong, both so self-assured, so confident in what they wanted out of life that they'd taken a chance. Ann had taken a chance on creating her business and another one on letting Lewis close enough to be a good friend after the heartache with her fiancé. Look how well that had turned out. What if she let Eric in all the way and he trampled her heart?

She turned to take out the glasses and begin filling them with ice. When she reached for the gallon tea pitcher and stepped back with it, she walked on Eric's foot. "Sorry!"

He steadied her with his hands at her waist. "Trying to cripple me so I won't beat you at fishing?"

"Didn't know you fished with your toes," Ann said, acutely aware of the warmth of his touch.

"Fishing requires skill and patience. I use my toes and feet to help with balance while fighting to reel in those monster catches."

"Monster catches? Like the one that got away the last time you were here? I heard Nick and Chad talking about that."

"Hey, that fish really was huge. Bigger than both of theirs. Not my fault it broke the line."

"Uh huh."

"Your doubt will be proven wrong, tomorrow. Me against you. The one who brings in the biggest fish gets indefinite bragging rights."

"I already have that." Ann smiled sweetly.

"I've heard you're a legend, but I haven't seen any of your fish, sweetheart."

Ann grinned, realizing how much she was enjoying the exchange. "You will. Tomorrow morning, I'll show you what a champion does."

Eric held out his hand. "You're going to lose."

Ann slid her hand into his. *Why does this feel so right?* "Haven't lost yet."

"You've never done it with me."

"If you two will stop holding hands, we can eat now," Noah called out.

The moment lost, Ann quickly pulled away from Eric.

Everyone gathered around the oversize table on the enclosed back porch to polish off the steak and side dishes. Amelia patted her stomach when she finished her baked potato and said, "Chad and I were talking about possible baby names." She looked around the table. "We thought if it's a girl, we'd name her after Grandma, and if it's a boy, we'll name him Henry Noah after the finest grandfathers in the world."

Noah blinked and sniffled, then wiped his eyes. "Damn onions."

Henry beamed and shook Chad's hand. "Well done, Chad."

Ann bit her lip, happy for her sister, but a strange yearning formulated in her. She wanted the bliss Amelia and Abby had.

Eric leaned closer and lowered his voice. "You okay?"

"I'm fine," she whispered back, trying to squelch the longing.

"I know, but friends offer support in good times as well as bad."

"You'd probably be a great boyfriend." As soon as she said it, Ann realized how true it was. Eric was a thoughtful guy. "Why'd your last girlfriend and you break up?"

"She hated that I always beat her at fishing."

Ann laughed and then shook her head when her family looked her way. "Sorry, we're going fishing in the morning, and Eric was making whales out of minnows."

"You just wait. I'll prove you wrong."

"It'll be colder on the lake, so bundle up," Noah said.

"I'll keep her warm," Eric said.

When her sisters said in unison, "I'll bet you will," and gave the two of them knowing looks, Ann elbowed him.

"I meant I'll bring a blanket," he clarified.

Taking pity on him since he wasn't completely used to her sisters' teasing, Ann rose and began picking up plates. "Eric and I will clear the table. You all can do the washing." She carried a stack into the kitchen.

Returning for more dishes, she walked up to Amelia, put her hand on her shoulder, and said, "I'm so happy for you and Chad."

Amelia patted her hand. "Thank you, Sis."

"All right, I'm ready to win at poker. Who's playing?" Henry asked. He waved his hand at Ann. "Let the dishes wait for a little while."

After a couple of rounds, Nick and Noah headed into the kitchen with Abby to clean up.

Ann packed up the cards and returned them to the closet, then sought out Eric. He was in the living room watching the way the moonlight rippled on the lake's water.

"Ready for bed, honey?" she joked. But once the words were out she realized how much she'd liked saying them.

He turned and gave her a smile that made her heart do a strange flip. "Finally! I thought you'd never ask." Without warning, he charged at her and flung her over his shoulder in a fireman's carry.

"Put me down." Ann laughed and slapped his back. "Do

you know what my Granddaddy is going to think?"

"Don't worry, I'm on the lookout for anyone who looks capable of performing a marriage ceremony. I'll give you enough of a warning so we can run." Eric walked into the bedroom and tossed her gently onto the top bunk before turning away. "I'm going to shower."

"Hey! The hot water can be wonky. Don't take it all."

As he walked out the door, Ann heard him mutter, "I'm going to take a cold shower. A *very* cold one."

Chapter Eleven

At five in the morning, he wasn't usually at his best, but add in a night of tossing and turning, and it was even worse. Eric looked at his bleary-eyed expression in the mirror above the sink and debated whether or not to shave, then decided to skip it. He could always do it later. He glanced toward the closed bathroom door when he heard steps in the hallway. How Ann had bounced out of bed all smiles with a the-world-is-beautiful attitude he'd never know. But then again, she hadn't stayed awake into the wee hours like he had.

The problem was that he'd been acutely aware of each breath she took. He'd gotten a glimpse of her in a silky, short pajama set, and he'd thought his damn tongue would loll out. Lying in the darkened room last night with only the pale moon for company, he'd tried everything to stop thinking of Ann, but it hadn't worked. Then his mind had dwelled on ways to make Lewis face up to what he'd done to her. Eric was determined not to let him make Ann the fall girl. He despised con men, but especially ones who used women. He couldn't imagine taking advantage of a woman financially or otherwise.

Before he'd do something like that or compromise his integrity in any way, he'd take a job flipping burgers until his hair turned gray and his teeth fell out. Shaking his head, he opened the door and nearly ran into Ann. Dressed in a pair of slim-fitting jeans and a long-sleeved shirt, she looked refreshed and ready to go.

Beaming at him, she offered a steaming cup of coffee. "You look grouchy. I take it you're not a morning person."

"I didn't sleep well."

She patted his arm. "You didn't have to spend the night tossing and turning worrying about losing. I promise I won't boast too much when I land the biggest fish."

"I'm an expert at fishing."

"Oh, yeah? Did a lot of it growing up?"

"No."

"I did. I went fishing all the time with Granddaddy. In fact, one summer, I spent all my allowance on fishing gear."

"If this is you trash talking, you need to try harder. You don't scare me, Ann."

She started humming the theme from *Jaws*. "Just when you thought it was safe to go back in the water…"

"Tell you what, whoever lands the biggest fish has to cook supper for a week for the other person."

She looked thoughtful. "I don't know, Eric. I'll be so busy trying to work a miracle with your bad boy changes, I won't have much time left over to do things like cook."

"Now that, woman, is trash talk, which can sometimes be misconstrued as flirting. Careful, or I might start to think that you're interested in me." He said it before he could stop himself. Could he dare hope that she was beginning to have an interest in him?

"I'm not flirting." Her eyes narrowed. "Losing sleep has interfered with your ability to think straight. What makes you think I'm interested in you?"

His heart dropped at her words. She definitely didn't sound interested. Quite the opposite. She sounded like she didn't care at all. "You pushed against me when we kissed at your shop."

"I did not."

He wasn't going to let that go. He might not be able to figure out why she'd responded to him the way that she had, but she'd been into the kiss. "Oh, yeah. There was pushing."

"You imagined it."

"Then you ran your hand under my shirt." He pulled the edge of his T-shirt free of the waist of his jeans.

She glanced down at the movement, then slowly back up. "I was only trying to get into the spirit of things."

"I know what you were trying to get into." He smirked. "Plus, you did ask me to kiss you."

Ann threw her hands up in the air. "Okay, you're right. I give. I was flirting, and I did ask you to kiss me. But running into my ex made me remember how I always mess up when it comes to men. Now are we going fishing or not?"

Eric leaned against the doorjamb. He couldn't help the smile even though his heart was pounding. They were on the brink of something. He could sense it. "Ann Snyder finally admits a partial truth to herself. So if you're interested, let's take this to the next step."

"What step?"

"Once we get your case settled, let's go on a date."

"I can't."

"Can't or won't?"

"Won't."

"I never took you for a coward, Ann."

"Yeah, well, when it comes to men, I'll be a coward and keep my heart safe, thanks."

"Do you know why I said partial truth? Because the

whole truth is that I think your heart is already leaning my way, isn't it?"

"The truth is that I'm going to grab my gear and get on the boat. If you're coming with me, I'll see you at the dock."

Eric smiled, and Ann made a noise of disgust before she marched out of the house. He caught the screen door before it could slam and wake the others. That was definitely something to think about. Could it be possible that he'd read the situation wrong all these years and she had been interested in him? Could he have missed something that monumental? That would certainly put a new twist on things.

He poured the thermos full of coffee and grabbed his jacket, making sure his cell phone was in the pocket. After picking up a blanket and a couple of breakfast bars, he headed out after Ann. Since he'd already loaded his gear last night, he didn't have to worry about lugging that along.

Ann was at the dock already untying the boat when he reached her.

"Are you driving, or do you want me to?" she asked.

"You drive out, I'll drive in." He climbed into the boat and stowed the blanket and the thermos before slipping his jacket on. The breeze blowing across the lake made the temperature a lot cooler.

"Which one did you bring?" she asked with a nod toward his gear.

"Which one? I brought my rod, why?"

Ann smirked. "I have a big collection of freshwater casting rods, saltwater rods, fly fishing rods. I didn't bring them all. Just a couple of my best freshwater ones."

"I guess you really are a fan of fishing."

"Granddaddy needed someone to go with him, and I always volunteered. More for him at first, than for myself. But the more I went, the more I enjoyed it."

"Really? Why?"

"There's nothing like the solitude and the peace of fishing when you need to clear your head."

"Did you need to clear your head a lot?"

She made a face and then sighed. "Especially right after my parents died. Everything changed so fast. Abby was working at the diner all the time because Granddaddy and Grandma were lost. They were both so depressed that it scared me. Amelia thought it was her fault, since our parents were returning home from their date to be with her."

"What about you?"

She gave a shaky laugh. "Can't believe I'm sharing all this. I don't usually talk about it."

"Talking about things instead of keeping them bottled up can help. Who better to listen than a great friend like me?"

Ann smiled at that, then her smile slowly faded. "When I learned about my parents' death, I remember feeling like I couldn't breathe at first. I kept on following Abby's lead, trying to keep on going, keep on with the day-to-day living, and then one day, I could breathe again." She glanced at him. "What about your family?"

"They're all screwed up. I'm the normal one."

Ann rolled her eyes. "If you say so."

"You'll discover that for yourself when you're cooking for me."

"Right. Like that's going to happen." She steered the boat to an area of the lake and then silenced the motor. "I see you brought a blanket to hide your shame for when I land the biggest catch."

"Poke fun all you want to, but it's time for you to prove it."

Eric put the bait on his rod and cast into the water, then leaned back and reached for the thermos. He poured himself a cup, then offered to do the same for her.

• • •

The awareness she felt when his fingers touched hers jolted her more fully awake better than an entire pot of coffee. Her heart beat faster and not just from the touch. Like a veil had been ripped from her eyes, she was seeing him more clearly than she ever had.

She took the cup and smiled, glad he didn't have the ability to read her mind. He looked so damned sexy with that five o'clock shadow. For the life of her, she still couldn't see why he thought he needed her help. Sure, he'd needed a little guidance in the clothing department, but as far as she could tell, Eric had a lot of positives going for him. Any woman would be lucky to have him—except she hated the thought of another woman being with him.

He'd suggested that they go on a date. She frowned at the thought and sent him a side-eye glance. Was he playing her? Her mind didn't think so, but her heart wasn't sure. Could she trust him? "I need to know something. Are you playing a game with me?"

"What?"

"When you said we should date. Are you playing mind games?"

He looked offended. "What kind of a question is that?"

"A legitimate one, given my history with men." She took a breath. "So if you're playing games, be up front with me."

"Be up front with you?"

She nodded and took a sip of the coffee.

"You want up front?" He leaned forward and put his elbows on his knees. "I'm interested in you. I've *always* been interested in you. Now it's your turn to do what you've always done. Create a long list of reasons why it'd never work out. You know why you like bad boys? Because you deliberately choose men who are wrong for you."

"Why would I do that?"

"Because that's the kind of guy you've always chosen. You pick a man who'll use you and has no hope in hell of ever being the kind who'll stick around for you. You do it because you're scared."

"You're wrong. I don't do it on purpose. I've sworn off men because I'm not about to be taken advantage of again." Feeling defensive, she shot him an irritated look. "Why would I pick guys like that?"

"Because you know if you pick a good guy, you might end up in a committed relationship."

"I was in a committed relationship. Are you forgetting I was engaged?"

"It was the worst night of my life when I found out you were engaged." His gaze assessed her. "He wasn't the right guy for you."

"I supposed you have an opinion on who would be the right guy? Let me guess. You."

"Like your best fantasy, sweetheart."

The breath she'd been holding suddenly escaped, and Ann felt as if she couldn't draw in enough oxygen. "It would never work. You don't know me."

"Because you won't let me. A few guys screw up, and the rest of the men in the world get written off."

"No, not a few guys, Eric. *All* of them. Including you. I haven't forgotten about the fantasy girl draft."

"What about it?"

"One of your friends suggested putting me on the list and you said I didn't belong, that I wasn't in the same class with those girls."

"So? You weren't." *Ouch.*

"You didn't think I was pretty enough in high school or after. I overheard you with Jerry. That's why you were written off. I don't want to be with someone who doesn't think

I'm enough. You with your sexiness and your unnecessary makeover and—" To her horror, Ann burst into tears.

"Oh my God, Ann. No. That fantasy draft was created about girls who were…"

While he searched for the right word, Ann said, "Beautiful?"

"Easy. Ones who had a reputation for going all the way on a first date. I knew you weren't like that. I didn't want them to think of you that way. As far as not being pretty enough, I can still remember how I felt the first time I saw you walk down the hallway. I was so stunned by your beauty I literally lost my breath. I choked on my gum."

Eric moved closer, causing the boat to gently rock. He wrapped his arms around her.

"Everyone always noticed my sisters. They're so beautiful and talented and—"

"I didn't even know you had sisters until I heard about your parents' car accident."

It was because of *her*? Ann put her head on his chest, inhaling the scent of his cologne and maleness. Taking a deep, steadying breath, she lifted her head and wiped at her eyes. "I'm afraid you'll hurt me."

He looked shocked. "Ann, I would never hurt you."

She waved her hand. "I know that you'd never hurt me physically. But what about my heart?"

He traced the path of her tears with his thumb. "The last thing in the world I'd ever want to do is to cause you heartache. Breaking your heart would break my own in return." Leaning in, he lowered his head slowly, taking the time to look into her eyes. Then he kissed her, sweetly, tenderly. "Why don't we at least give it a shot? Go on a date with me. If, at the end of the date, you don't want to move forward, I'll back off, and that'll be the end of it. We'll be friends, okay?"

Ann swallowed. She was scared, but the fear that she was

making a mistake was outweighed by her feelings for Eric.

"Great. When we get back—" The shrill of his telephone cut off what he was about to say. He held up a finger and answered it.

Ann took a deep, shuddering breath. This was it. There was a fork in the road in her relationship with Eric, and she'd veered onto the side she'd normally never have chosen with him. But she'd played it safe for too long. She liked him, and Eric wasn't like her jerk ex-fiancé. He wasn't a con man like Lewis. He was honorable, courageous, and oh-so-tempting.

He ended the phone call and blew out a breath. "Some good news. I met with the private investigator yesterday morning. Lewis has been located, and the agents investigating your case are now aware of this information."

Relief and hope racing through her, Ann clapped her hands. "Will the police bring him back here?"

"No. He hasn't officially been charged with a crime, so they don't have any cause. But don't worry. I'll handle getting him back here."

"He's not going to come willingly."

"I'll make sure he's asked very nicely. Hey, I've got a bite." Eric grabbed his rod when the tip bobbed down and began to reel in the line. "There's a nice restaurant not far from the lake house. We could get dinner there tonight."

Plucking at her jeans, Ann said, "I didn't bring anything but jeans with me."

He glanced at her. "So?"

"So I want to look nice."

He grinned. "If you're thinking that you want to dress up to impress me, you can forget it. I'm already impressed with you."

Ann giggled, then covered her mouth.

Eric pulled in the end of his broken fishing line and sighed. "I have the worst luck with fishing lines. What?" He swiveled to look at her.

"I can't believe I giggled. I don't giggle. It's so weird. I feel like I'm back in high school." She reached for the end of the line and examined it. "How old is your line?"

"A few years. It was old the last time I went fishing with Nick and Chad." He brushed her hair away from her face.

Ann's skin tingled. "Um…you need new line. See? You have several nicks here. It happens when the line runs across the teeth of the fish. You should change the line every season and a more expensive brand will last longer, too."

"I'll defer to your expertise the next time I buy supplies. You can help me pick them out."

"Did you bring any extra fishing line? I can replace it now if you did."

"No, I didn't."

"Too bad. Then I guess you won't be able to catch the biggest fish after all."

Eric shrugged. "Doesn't matter to me. You agreeing to go on a date with me makes everything else insignificant."

She ducked her head. "You really know how to flatter a girl."

"I'm not flattering you. I'm being honest."

"If we're being honest here, tell me why you really wanted me to do a makeover that you didn't really need."

He hesitated, then said, "You always seemed to choose the bad boy type. I thought if I tried to become that kind of guy, you'd see me in a different light and hopefully be attracted to me."

She put her hand on the side of his face to turn his head toward her when he winced and looked away. "The bad boys I've had in my life have all been self-centered jerks who put their own needs first. I don't think you have it in you to be anything close to that."

"No?"

"No." Leaning closer, Ann softly kissed him. "But if you're referring to being the kind of guy who's breathtakingly good looking, the kind that women can't help but want, then you are definitely that kind of guy."

"Is that so?"

She tugged at the collar of his shirt. "Yes. Even when you used to wear those bow ties."

"I wore the bow ties, because I would go to the pediatric cancer ward at the hospital. There was a kid there who's a big *Doctor Who* fan. He wanted some bow ties. I brought them to him, and he asked me if I'd wear them, too. So I did."

Ann blinked back tears. "Wow. Is the kid okay?"

Eric nodded. "I keep in touch with the family, and his father said he's doing well."

Ann's stomach rumbled. She pressed a hand against her abdomen. "Sorry. I'm hungry. You are not who I thought you were."

He grinned. "Didn't Lois Lane say the same thing to Clark Kent?""

Ann laughed.

"Let's head back and get something to eat." He stowed his rod while Ann did the same.

As soon as she was settled, he powered the boat back the way that they'd come.

With the chilly wind on her face as they headed back, Ann relaxed. Lewis had been located, and she had a date with a great guy. It looked like the nightmare about her business was going to end well. Things were finally turning around for her.

Chapter Twelve

That evening, shortly after six, with the wide-eyed grin of Noah following them out of the lake house, Eric walked toward the van. He was as nervous as he'd been the first time he'd tried a case. Now, as then, he'd probably over prepared, changing his clothes repeatedly, pacing the room, hoping he didn't screw up. He couldn't believe that he had a date with Ann.

He opened the passenger door for her and helped her in. "You're beautiful, Ann."

She patted the thighs of her jeans. "It's my high-end clothes you're seeing."

"I have twenty-twenty vision when it comes to you." He smiled as the color flooded her face.

The drive to the small restaurant didn't take long, but because it was one of the more popular ones in the area, Eric had to park at the far end of the parking lot.

Ann shivered when something rustled in the bushes beside the restaurant, and she scooted closer to him.

"Not a fan of nature?" he asked.

"I'm a big fan of nature. I'm just not a fan of anything with more teeth than I have."

He slung his arm around her shoulders. "I'll protect you. Unless we go swimming and encounter a shark. Then it's every man for himself."

She laughed and lightly smacked his chest. "Are you afraid of sharks?"

"Not at all. Their bites on the other hand…" He opened the door for her and waited for her to walk in. "Don't tell me you're not afraid of them."

"Not sharks. Bears. I always have those dreams where I'm being chased by a bear."

Eric gave their name to the hostess, and then the two took a seat on the bench to wait for a table. "You know what I admire about you with your business situation?" He glanced at her and went on. "Even though Lewis wronged you, I haven't heard you talk about revenge or even speak ill about him. You have a kind heart, Ann."

She leaned back and crossed her legs. "You say that because you don't know how often I played a mental game of Hangman featuring Lewis as the stick figure."

Eric laughed.

"I was thinking that even if Lewis is brought back and confesses to what he did, the money he swindled from people is probably long gone. So I made the decision to pay those people back every cent even if I have to work the rest of my life to do it."

"As your friend, I admire that. As your attorney, I wouldn't advise you to make that move right now until I get things settled. It could make you look guilty."

"Friends. I like the sound of that," she admitted.

Eric shifted on the bench and wrapped his arm around her shoulders. "Me, too. How do you plan to pay the people back?"

"I'm going to sell my house. It's in a sought-after neighborhood, so it shouldn't take too long. Then I'll sell my car. I'm going to talk to Abby about letting me stay on at the diner until I can start up the business again. I won't need a car because I can walk back and forth to my shift if I stay with Grandfather."

"If you sell your home and can't stay with your grandfather, you'll need a place to live."

"I'll think of something. Life's an adventure, right?"

"Right." He rose when the hostess came to lead them to a table. Eric settled himself after Ann was seated and raised his eyebrows at her expression. "What?"

"You know how we talked about not really knowing each other?" She moved the kerosene lamp carefully from the center of the table and set it to the side.

He nodded.

Ann rubbed a spot on the palm of her hand and then looked up at him. "We can change that. You tell me some things about yourself, and I'll tell you things about me. It has to be something the other person doesn't know."

Eric liked the idea of getting to know more about Ann. "Okay, you start. Tell me something about yourself."

The waitress approached and greeted them, then took their drink orders. As soon as she was gone, Ann said, "This isn't life-altering information, but I always watch a sitcom before I go to bed. The laughter helps me to relax. I've done it since I was a kid. Your turn—something serious."

"Let's see… I snuck out of the house when I was fourteen to go on a camping trip with my friends. Three days passed before anyone in my house knew I was gone."

"That's terrible."

"I was thankful to have those three days of peace and didn't see it as a bad thing that no one looked for me right away."

"I had the opposite problem," Ann confessed. "After my parents died, Abby become so protective. She was always breathing down my neck. I resented her actions then, but I didn't realize she became that way because she was afraid of losing me and Amelia."

Eric slid his arm across the table and took her hand, but the waitress returned before he could tell her how much he wished he could erase all her heartache. He gave his order and waited until Ann gave hers. Once the waitress left them alone again, he said, "I can't imagine what you all went through."

"There are times when the pain isn't as deep. But when I think about my mom not being here for the day I get married or my dad not being around to be a grandfather to any children I might have, then the hurt feels just as fresh as ever."

"That's understandable."

She linked her fingers with his. "You said you don't have a good relationship with your parents?"

"My mother tried to be a good mom, but she's an alcoholic. The drinking made her zone out of all of our lives when I was about eight."

"I'm sorry, Eric. I had no idea."

He shrugged, not wanting her to feel sorry for him. Life was what it was. "No one else knows. My family has kept it pretty quiet. Anyway, on a lighter note, if you could travel anywhere in the world, where would you go?"

Ann closed her eyes and a smile played on her lips. She opened her eyes. "Everywhere. I love to travel, but I always come back. Sweet Creek is home. It's where I hope to someday raise a family."

"But if there was one special place you could go, where would it be?"

"Alaska."

He rubbed his chin. "That's not what I was expecting. I thought you'd pick somewhere exotic."

"I've always wanted to visit Alaska."

"It's cold."

She wiggled her eyebrows. "Not if you know how to stay warm."

He laughed, encouraged by the expression on her face. "Are you flirting with me?"

"Not very well if you have to ask."

"So you want to raise a family in Sweet Creek."

"That's the plan. I'd like to have six or seven kids."

He nearly sputtered into his drink. "Uh...are you serious?"

She grinned. "No, but you should see your face."

The waitress returned with Eric's fish and Ann's lasagna. After she left, Eric said, "Did you ever imagine that the two of us would be on a date?"

• • •

Ann took a sip of her drink and set the glass back down carefully, wondering how much she should say. If she said too much, she would reveal a vulnerable side she wasn't sure she was comfortable sharing. She opened her mouth to say something funny and breezy but then her eyes locked with his. Swallowing, she said, "Yes."

He stopped cutting his roll in half. "You did?"

"I used to imagine pulling off that plaid bow tie and kissing you, wondering what your reaction would be."

"You acted like you couldn't stand to be around me."

"I was reacting from the belief that you were playing some kind of game, and that hurt."

He looked stunned. "What changed?"

"I realized on the boat earlier that I was playing it safe because of how I'd been hurt, and I'm ready to risk it again. With you."

Eric carefully wiped his mouth. "I want to be with you Ann, and I'm not talking about short term either."

Ann smiled, her heart soaring. The rest of the meal passed in a blur. When they were finished, Eric asked, "Do you want to get out of here?"

Ann was more than ready. Breathless, she nodded, managing to squeak out, "Yes." From the look in his eyes, she knew exactly where this was headed. But there was no dread in the pit of her stomach. No hesitation. She wanted to be with Eric.

He waited while she slid out from the table, and when she stood beside him, he put his hand at the small of her back. Ann reveled in the warm guidance from his hand. They stopped at the front to pay the bill and walked to the door.

The second they stepped outside, the world erupted into bright flashes of light, momentarily blinding Ann and filling her with confusion. The lights were quickly followed by shouted questions as, like wild animals, people seemed to spring from every corner. Ann was reminded of a feeding frenzy she'd once seen on a shark documentary.

The men and women swarming around the restaurant carried bulky cameras and pressed against them, blocking Ann's path.

One voice shouted out, "Miss Snyder, is it true you convinced people that your chocolates could cure various diseases?"

Then another one, "Any comment about the investment scheme fraud charges?"

Eric put his arm around her waist, snapped out, "No comment," and rushed Ann toward the van.

She climbed in on the driver's side with Eric quickly following after her. He put the van into gear and spun out of the parking lot.

Turning around in the seat, Ann watched as the group

continued to take photos. "How did they know where I was?"

"They can smell a story a mile away." He reached across the console for her hand. "Trust me. Everything will be fine. I promise."

Though she was still on edge, Ann decided that she could trust Eric. "Okay."

He glanced at her. "They sure killed the mood, didn't they?"

She laughed. "A little."

"Despite the wild-eyed photographers showing up, I had a good time tonight."

"Me, too."

"Think you'd like to do it again?"

"Definitely."

Back at the lake house, she shared with her family what had happened.

"What a rotten way to end a date," Amelia said.

"No good night kiss," Nick added.

"Grandkids interruptus," Noah said glumly, and everyone laughed.

"We should start the campfire. It's a beautiful night," Abby said.

The way her sister's eyes sparkled made Ann pause. She narrowed her eyes. "You look awfully happy about something. Am I going to be an aunt twice already?"

"No, nothing like that." Some of the joy faded from Abby's face.

Ann wanted to kick herself, hating that she'd reminded her sister of the loss she'd experienced. "Sorry."

"It's fine." Abby waved a hand. "Nick's brother Elliot called. He's going to be in town for Thanksgiving."

"I didn't know he was going to be able to make it, so I invited his wife," Nick said.

Ann whistled. From what she'd heard, the separated

couple wasn't exactly on speaking terms. "Guess we can expect fireworks for the Thanksgiving meal, then."

"Probably." Nick motioned toward Eric and Chad. "Let's get the firewood set up."

"We'll help," Henry offered and shuffled forward slowly beside Noah.

As soon as the sisters were alone, Amelia said, "So spill. Besides the paparazzi how was the date?"

Ann didn't even have to think about it. "Really good. Eric is easy to talk to and he's funny and he's— Why the looks?"

"You're into him, aren't you?" Abby looked delighted.

"Yes." Ann gave in, tired of fighting herself. "I always was, but I didn't want to admit it. Whenever he's around, my heart races. I look forward to seeing him, and he's such a giving person and he does all these wonderful things and he's sexy and…" Ann stopped talking and sighed. "I'm in trouble, aren't I?"

"Sounds like love to me." Amelia took a bag of marshmallows from the pantry.

"I would have to agree." Abby picked her jacket up from the table and slipped it on.

"Love? No. It's a crush. I don't love Eric." Ann bit her fingernail. She *didn't* love Eric. Wasn't in love with him. If she loved him, she'd know that she was in love with him, right?

"You bite your nails when you're nervous," Amelia pointed out and holding the bag of marshmallows, left the room.

"Abby, I can't love Eric."

Her sister gave her a gentle smile. "The heart doesn't listen to the reasons why we shouldn't let love in. It simply loves."

No. It couldn't be. Ann trailed after her sister. She wasn't ready to be in love. Especially with Eric. She stopped abruptly when she saw him seated by the campfire laughing at something her grandfather had said. The fire cast a warm glow over his face. He was honest. Kind. Handsome. He made her blood sing when he kissed her. Made her believe in fairy tales.

Eric looked over at her and motioned her toward him, patting a space on the log beside him. Ann moved forward, unable to look away. Her heart was a moment away from falling for Eric and this time, she wasn't going to stop it from happening. She was going to fall and take a chance.

Chapter Thirteen

The Monday afternoon after they'd all returned from the lake house, Eric received the good news he'd hoped for. He ended the phone call and pumped his fist into the air, earning a raised eyebrow from his secretary, but he didn't care.

Lewis had confessed to setting Ann up, and once restitution was made, she would be off the hook. Since it would take a while to fight the IRS for the return of her money—and even then there was no guarantee that they'd win—Eric had taken a different avenue to get Ann back in business before it was too late for her company.

The weekend at the lake house had been like a dream to him. The date with Ann, the closeness had fed into the hope that there was a future for the two of them. Tonight, he would take her out for a romantic dinner and tell her how he felt about her. If all the stars aligned in his favor, maybe she'd tell him she felt the same way.

He drove to the diner, parked, and went in to find her. She was waiting on a table, pencil poised above her order pad, her beautiful face wreathed in a smile.

Sliding into one of the booths, he waited until she'd finished the order and fastened the ticket to the carousel. When she turned around, she spotted him and her smile widened. She hurried over to the table. "Hi," she greeted softly.

"Sit for a second."

Ann sat across from him. "What's up?"

"I didn't want to say anything before we left for the trip to the lake house in case it fell through, but it's over."

She leaned forward. "It is?"

Eric reached into the pocket of his suit coat and slid an envelope toward her. "Here's your money back as well as interest. You're free to open up the shop. There will be a trial down the road, and you might have to testify against Lewis."

"Gladly." She opened the envelope, then frowned. "This is a cashier's check from your bank."

"I figured it would be easier for your bank to take a cashier's check."

"I can pay you for the case now," she offered.

He shook his head. "We had a deal."

She ducked her head.

Eric reached across the table and tipped her face upward. "Are you okay?"

"I'm fine. Really. Feeling a little overwhelmed. I should get back to work."

"I'm meeting Chad and Nick, so I'll be hanging out here for a little while. Will I be in your way?"

"Not at all." Ann scooted out of the booth and smoothed down her apron. She reached for Eric's hand and gave it a squeeze. "Thank you."

Eric nodded, squishing the small voice within him that said she wouldn't like how he'd been able to give her the money. The bottom line was that he'd given Ann back the business she loved. That's all that mattered to him.

"I'd better get back to helping Abby, but I'll see you

tonight."

"How about I take you out to dinner? Some place romantic?"

"Sounds good."

He watched her go, feeling satisfied with his life all because he'd made her happy. He'd barely had time to take a sip of his coffee before Nick and Chad joined him.

"You said you had news," Chad said.

"Ann's case is finished. Lewis confessed, and he'll be charged. She's off the hook."

"What about her business?"

"She can open up again."

"How? She doesn't have any funds, and she refused to take any from her sisters or me." Chad turned over a cup and raised his hand to get the waitress over to fill it with coffee.

"You gave her your money, didn't you?" Nick asked. When Eric nodded, Nick said, "Did you tell her it was your money?"

"There's no need to. When Lewis has to make restitution, I'll get the money back then."

"It was a lot of money," Nick said. "Probably the majority of everything you had socked away. Did you cash in your retirement account?"

"So?" Eric lifted his coffee cup and took a drink. When he set it down, he said, "I love her, and I want her to be happy. If I can protect her from having to close up her shop because of Lewis, then I will."

"Let me tell you something about women." Chad rubbed the side of his face. "They don't see omissions as a man being protective. They see it as being lied to."

Eric frowned. "But I didn't lie."

"You kept it from her." Nick picked up a menu and scanned the contents before looking back at Eric. "Even though I was doing something nice for Abby by fixing up the diner's extension behind her back, it didn't go over well."

"He's right. Take it from our screw-ups. The Snyder women like everything up front. The clearer the better."

Eric glanced toward the kitchen when he heard the sound of Ann's laughter. He leaned forward across the table and brought his index finger and thumb together. "I'm this close to telling Ann how I feel about her." He shook his head. "I fixed her problems, so what's the big deal?"

"Hope you like the doghouse, man," Nick said, and he and Chad bumped fists.

"I remember being stupid about Amelia and nearly lost her because I thought I was right. Tell her what happened," Chad said.

Eric glanced at the kitchen again, then back at his friends. "I can't. We're in a place I've dreamed of for years." His friends were wrong. He didn't need to tell Ann it was his money. She was happy, and that was all that mattered.

• • •

Ann chopped vegetables for the soup Abby was making, humming under her breath as she did. When she dumped the carrots and beans into the pot and turned around, her sisters were grinning at her.

She grinned back. "I was humming, I know, but I can't help it. I can reopen the shop."

Amelia and Abby nudged each other. "And that's the only reason you're humming? It doesn't have anything to do with a handsome six-foot-something guy sitting with our husbands?" Amelia said.

"It does. Eric isn't like the men I've known in the past. He's great and I..." She sighed and pressed a hand over her heart. "I'm tired of denying it. I love him. I think I have for a while, but I was so caught up in the pain I'd experienced that

I wouldn't acknowledge it to myself."

Her sisters squealed with delight and rushed to envelop her in a group hug.

"When are you going to tell him?"

"Tonight. We're going out for dinner. I'll tell him after that. I never imagined feeling this happy and especially not with Eric."

The sisters hugged once more before getting back to work.

For Ann, the rest of the day seemed to drag by. She couldn't wait to see Eric. To look into his amazing eyes and tell him what was in her heart. Given all that she'd been through with men, she wouldn't deny that there was some trepidation, some risk, but this was Eric. The risk was small in comparison.

When she dropped a second glass because she couldn't keep her mind on what she was supposed to be doing, her sisters ordered her out of the diner and told her to get ready for her big night.

Ann promised to call them as soon as she could and hopped into her Volkswagen. She'd splurge for a new dress and shoes. She wanted to remember this night forever as a night of new beginnings. Who knew where it might lead? She couldn't stop smiling as she ran her errands.

At the little dress shop she loved but normally couldn't afford, she picked out a vintage floral dress and paired it with mint green heels. She paid for her purchases, then hurried toward his condo, wanting to beat Eric home.

She let herself in and set the packages on the sofa, then went to take a shower and get ready for what was sure to be the best night of her life.

• • •

Ann, as usual, looked fantastic. He was sure he looked like a nervous wreck. Which was exactly what he was. He'd had time to think over what Nick and Chad had told him, and he knew they were right. Coming clean with Ann was necessary. He wished it wasn't so hot in the restaurant. He felt like he was beneath a spotlight with all his faults waiting to be exposed.

"That's the third time you've tugged at the collar of your shirt. Did we buy the wrong size?" Ann asked.

Eric lowered his hand and picked up his glass, then set it back down without taking a sip. "No. It's not the clothes. I need to tell you something."

Her face lit up. "I want to tell you something, too."

"Go ahead."

She reached for his hand. "I don't know how it happened or even when. It's not like I can pinpoint it. Maybe it goes all the way back to high school. I don't know. Funny, too, because the whole time I thought—" She stopped and blushed. "I'm babbling. Sorry."

He stroked his thumb across the back of her hand. "What do you want to say?"

"I love you."

Eric blinked. *Did she… Had she just said…* He swallowed, unable to stop staring at her.

Uncertainty crossed her face, and she bit her lip.

"I'm officially a believer in miracles." He pushed back his chair and walked over to her. "I love you."

"You love me?"

He loved the radiance in her eyes. "From the beginning of time to the end." Pulling her against him, he covered her mouth with his until he thought he'd go mad with the need to be alone with her. Raising his head, he said, "I'm hungry, but not for food."

"Me, too."

Eric pulled a few bills from his wallet and tossed them on the table to cover their drinks, then led the way to the door.

Hand in hand, they walked to his car and got in. Eric started the car and turned on the heater to warm up the interior. He'd tell Ann about the money tomorrow. He wanted to spend the night with her. The fact that she loved him was beyond his wildest dreams, and he didn't want to do or say anything to mess that up.

• • •

The next morning, Ann was in Eric's kitchen making pancakes when he approached her. He was freshly showered, his dark hair still wet with water. He kissed the side of her neck, and Ann shivered.

He reached around her for a piece of bacon waiting on a plate. "Sleep well?" he asked, his deep voice ripe with meaning.

"What sleep I did get was pretty amazing." She pushed his hand away. "Get dressed, and we can eat. I have something I want to run by you."

"Okay." He winked at her and disappeared down the hall.

She hadn't known it was possible to be this happy. To think she'd poked fun of her sisters and what she'd thought of as their newlywed mushiness. What an idiot she'd been. They'd known what she didn't. That when the right man came along, it made all the difference in the world.

Eric returned dressed in a pair of jeans and one of the pullover shirts she'd helped him pick out. "Not going to the office today?"

"No, I am." He shrugged. "Thought I'd be casual today. I sure feel a lot more relaxed than I have in ages." Putting his hands on her shoulders, he said, "You cooked. Sit, and I'll serve us."

Ann took a seat at the table while Eric put the pancakes and bacon in the center. He added syrup and a carton of orange juice, then sat across from her. "I hope what you want to run by me involves a lot more nights like last night."

She grinned. "If you're lucky." Reaching for the syrup, she poured some to the side of the pancakes. "I want to wait a week before I open up the shop again. In the meantime, I was thinking of taking a trip. The two of us. What do you think?"

"I'm anywhere that you are, Ann."

She reached for his hand. "I feel so…"

"Like the world is a better place?"

"Yeah. Like that. Anyway…" She picked up a napkin. "I was thinking that we could visit Alaska. Or we can decide on a different location if you don't like that idea."

"Alaska's fine with me, because it's fine with you."

"Great." She ducked her head and smiled. "I'm going to go by the shop to pick up some paperwork."

"Want company? I can go into the office late."

"That's a bad idea. I can't concentrate when you're around."

He made a cross-my-heart motion. "I'll behave."

She rolled her eyes. "Don't you remember what happened the last time we were at my shop together?"

"Do I remember? I think about it every time I see those iced French vanilla coffees at the store."

She laughed softly. "Me, too."

He leaned toward her and kissed her. "I love you."

"I love you, too."

Chapter Fourteen

Eric drove to his office and did his best to concentrate on his caseload. All he could think about was Ann and what she meant to him. He'd wait until they were on the trip and tell her about the money. No…he'd tell her before they took the trip in case she did get upset. It was only money. Surely she wouldn't be mad at him for trying to help. Of course she wouldn't.

That afternoon when his secretary announced that his mother was in the waiting room, he quickly walked out to find her, hoping she was ready to tell him she was going back to rehab.

The look of pity on his secretary's face told him all he needed to know. He wrapped his arm around his mother's shoulders and ushered her into his office, closing the door behind him. She backed into a chair, then steadied herself, before easing down into it. "I ran into that girl today."

"What girl?"

"The case one. Ann. She was at the bank, and I talked to her."

"Okay, Mom. I'll call a cab for you, okay?"

"She was sad when I left."

That was Eric's first inkling that something was wrong. "What do you mean?"

"Well, she wasn't sad. Not at first." His mother shook her head vigorously. "I saw the check she had, and I asked her why in the world my son was giving her that kind of money." She touched the side of her nose. "I'm looking out for you."

"What did you do?"

"I told her that no self-respecting woman would take that kind of money from a guy unless she was using him. Well…" She crossed her legs and leaned back in the chair. "She told me it was her money, and she'd gotten it back. I had to straighten her out. Tell her that when someone steals your money, especially the amount I saw on that check, you have to sue them. Your lawyer doesn't just give it to you. Unless it's *his* money."

Eric's pulse raced. He had to get to Ann and explain before she thought the worst of him.

His mother wagged her finger. "I told her that your father could have made her case go away like that." She snapped her fingers. "But that you wouldn't let him."

Eric could only imagine what Ann thought. He rushed out to his secretary's desk. "Get a cab. Put my mother in it and send her to this address." He scribbled down the address of his childhood home and then ran out to his car. The entire way to Ann's shop, he prayed that it wasn't too late.

• • •

Ann rested her back against the display case. Eric could have prevented her case from reaching the level that it had and he'd lied to her about the money. What else had he lied to her about? She wiped her eyes with her hands, her heart full of questions and hurt. Why hadn't he just been honest with her? Had he used the case to get close to her? To make her fall in love with him? Had this been a joke at her expense? Why else would he have not used his father's connections to help her?

When someone knocked on the door, she debated for a second on whether or not to open it, then climbed to her feet. Eric. She watched him through the glass, and he tapped on the door.

"Ann, please let me in."

She unlocked the door and stepped back, dread resting heavily on her. "I drew up a design for a new truffle. Look. A heart. Then I went to the bank and ran into your mother."

She backed away when he reached for her. "You could have talked to your father about my case, and it would have gone away. But you didn't. Then you lied to me about the check." Walking over to the counter, she picked it up and held it out. "I couldn't deposit it after I knew the truth."

"Ann…"

"Please don't. I'm going to get my things from your condo. Just so you know, lying is the kind of thing that a bad boy does, so, um…congratulations. I'd say the lessons were a success."

If he thought she was going to collapse in a heap in front of him and beg him to tell her why he'd done what he had, he was wrong. She wouldn't give him the satisfaction. "I want you to leave."

"Ann, I wish—"

"Go."

As soon as the door closed behind him, Ann locked it and gave the key a savage twist. Jerk. She'd been right the whole time. He was exactly like the other men. No, he was the worst of them all. King of liars. He'd acted like he was different and then destroyed her. Once again, she'd proven that she always picked the kind of man who was wrong for her. But she didn't remember it ever hurting this much.

Ann walked back behind the counter. So it was over. She'd dust her hands of him and wouldn't give him another thought. Leaning against the wall, she slid to the floor in the spot where she and Eric had kissed. Putting her head on her knees, she closed her eyes and wept.

The shadows on the wall lengthened, the shop growing dark inside before Ann finally stood. Her muscles protested the movement. She licked her dry lips and drew in a ragged breath. When a movement by the door caught her eye, she jumped before realizing it was Abby.

Moving forward on feet that felt as if they were encased in iron, she unlocked the door.

"I've been calling you, and Amelia's been calling. We've been everywhere looking for you. I drove by the shop several times but didn't see your car."

"I parked behind it," Ann said, not surprised to hear how her voice croaked. "I heard the phone but I…I…"

Abby pulled her into a hug. "Circumstances aren't always what they seem. I know what Eric did."

"How?"

"He called to talk to Nick, but he sounded so awful that I kept talking to him, and he spilled what he'd done." Abby stepped back and rubbed her hands up and down Ann's arms. "I'm sure he has a reason behind it all."

"But what reason would he have to lie to me and think it's okay? To not use every possible advantage to help me with my case?"

"I won't pretend that I can ever be in the mindset of a man," Abby said with a grin.

"Well, I'll do what I've always done. Pick myself up and start over. I'll figure out a way to reopen the shop. I don't know how yet, but I will."

"Good for you. The best recipe for heartache, Sis, is to stay busy. Don't dwell on what he said or the reasons behind it, whatever they might be."

Ann shook her head while painful emotions danced together in her heart. "Will you go with me to get my things from his place?"

"Right beside you, Sis."

• • •

Three hours later, Eric was up to his elbows in paperwork at his family's office when the front door flung open and Nick and Chad marched in. Their anger was understandable. Even though it had been unintentional, he'd hurt Ann. "Go ahead. Let me have it. I know I deserve it."

His friends sat across from him, and Nick started with, "Do you have any idea the trouble you've caused for Chad and me?"

"No…" Eric frowned at them. "Why would this cause trouble for you two?"

"Because Abby asked me if I knew what was going on with you. I told her I did." He grimaced. "She's mad at me for keeping that from her."

Chad jerked a thumb toward his chest. "Same here. Amelia's mad at me. While it's bad enough when a woman is mad, when you add pregnancy hormones, she wants your head on a spear."

"What the hell is going on? Ann doesn't know the truth, only that you lied to her. Why didn't you tell her the reasons why you did what you did?" Nick demanded.

Eric dropped the pen he'd held and scrubbed his hands down his face. "I tried but she wouldn't listen. Then I saw her face, how hurt she was. I didn't want to push her. I figured she was lumping me in with the guys who disappointed her. I've never been so damn miserable in my life." He pounded his fist on the desk. "To be that close and then lose her…" His throat worked.

"You should have told her the truth," Nick said.

"But I didn't. I thought I had time." Eric held his arms out. "I wish there was something I could do."

"You can," Chad said in a quiet voice. "Let her in."

Eric looked away. Chad knew about his mother's alcoholism and how it had affected him. As a child, he'd learned to try and fix whatever unpleasant situation was going on. As a man, he still wanted to fix things, to change unpleasant situations and by not telling Ann where the money had come from, it had been a form of trying to control the situation. That was wrong of him. He'd known it but ignored that as well as the advice of his friends.

He slid back his chair. "I'm going to go after her."

• • •

Thanksgiving came and went. Two weeks before Christmas, Ann flipped through the order pad. Business had doubled from before she'd had the trouble with Lewis. She'd borrowed the money to open again from Chad and would pay him back after the court released the money the police had managed to recover from Lewis.

She should be happy, but she was miserable. The holidays made her miss Eric more. When the family had gathered to celebrate, she'd thought that Eric would be there. He usually at least stopped by, but there had been nothing.

Regardless, she wouldn't waste time grieving over him. She wasn't the type of woman to chase a man. Ann poured herself a cup of coffee and sat at her desk in the back of the shop. She'd take a few minutes to read the paper before she called more applicants in for the part-time position she needed to fill for the upcoming year.

She started to read the paper but couldn't concentrate.

Folding it, she tossed it aside. What was she doing? She'd never been a sit-on-the-sidelines woman. Eric owed her an explanation. Then, she'd have closure and be able to move on.

Ann grabbed her purse and headed for the front of the shop, stopping abruptly when the door opened and Eric walked in.

Her gaze ran hungrily over him. He looked tired, thinner than he had the last time she'd seen him.

"Hi," he said and took a deep breath.

"Why?" She had to know.

He didn't pretend not to know what she was talking about. "I had to protect you." He put his hands in his pockets. "I thought I was doing what was best. My father could have made your case go away. He could have made a few phone calls, greased a few palms, and the entire thing would have gone away." Eric took a step forward. "It's easy to take that first step when you convince yourself that you're right in your actions."

"What step?"

"Crossing from legal to illegal methods. I'm not a saint. Getting my father to make your case go away by whatever means necessary crossed my mind, but I knew I wouldn't be able to face myself later."

"I wouldn't have wanted you to do that anyway." She hadn't known what his father helping her would entail and she was relieved that Eric hadn't compromised his beliefs for her.

"I'm glad. About the check…I wanted to make you happy. I had the money and knew that eventually the case would settle, and I'd get it back."

"You lied to me."

He nodded. "I did, and I'm sorry. I'm not trying to make excuses for that, but I get uncomfortable when someone I love is hurting and I can't fix it. I do it with my mom. I want so badly for her to get help that I kept trying. I only recently realized that nothing is working, because I can't fix her." He exhaled. "And I can't fix your problems. I don't have the words to say to fix us. I would if I did."

"What are you saying?"

"I'm saying that whether there's an us is up to you. I would like that, but I won't try to fix something that you don't want fixed." He reached into the pocket of his jacket and withdrew an envelope. "I have a Christmas gift for you."

Ann took the envelope and opened it. A cruise ticket for Alaska. "You remembered."

"I remember everything you said. I have a matching ticket for myself." He shoved his hands into his pockets again. "The ship leaves from Vancouver the week after Christmas. Whatever you think about me…" His throat worked. "I want you to know that hurting you was the stupidest thing I've ever done. I don't really believe in miracles, but if there was any chance, any sliver of hope, that you could forgive me, then I would consider that a Christmas miracle."

When Ann didn't speak, Eric nodded. "I'll be waiting for you at the ship. If you don't show, then I'll know that this was good-bye." He pushed open the door and walked outside.

Dropping the ticket on the counter, Ann went after him. "That's it? You come into the shop and tell me that hurting me was so hard for you and that you want me to forgive you, but that's it?"

"I don't understand."

She shivered in the wind. "Days have gone by. You never called, never stopped by to try and talk to me."

He took off his jacket and held it out to her. "I didn't know what to do."

Ann slid her arms into his jacket and the familiar scent of him enveloped her.

She ignored the frustration in his voice. "I know that love

doesn't give up when things get tough."

"I never gave up."

"Yes, you did." Ann put her hands on her hips, growing angrier by the second. "You decided that there was no way you could trust me enough to be honest. That's not what partners do. People who love each other face life together whatever comes. You should have been honest with me. It makes me wonder if I can really trust you."

He threw his hands out. "If you want to use this to lump me in with all the other guys in your past, then go ahead. I'm not saying that I handled it the best way that it could've have been handled. I'm saying that I did my best to protect you, and I'm sorry for hurting you."

She shrugged out of his jacket and held it out to him. "I don't know what to think."

Eric took the jacket. "I have always loved you. I will always love you. Even if we can't ever be together, I'm a phone call away if you need anything at all. I'll drop everything to get to you."

Ann gritted her teeth to keep from crying. She wanted to rush to him, fling herself into his arms, tell him she was sorry for his family's pain, for his pain, but she was still hurting. And mixed up. And hurting. And mixed up. She bit her lip.

"I'll see you, Ann." He spun around and headed to the parking lot.

As she listened to his footsteps walk away, Ann couldn't help but think of how final they sounded.

Chapter Fifteen

Eric pulled the tape from the dispenser and fastened the strip across the top of another box. His mother had crashed a society function, thrown a glass of wine in the mayor's face, and this time, there was no hiding it from the world. It had shown up on newspapers all over the South. The mayor with wine dripping down his face. His father's horrified expression. Eric sighed and ran a hand across the back of his neck.

Unable to stand the public humiliation, his father had walked out and filed for divorce. His mother had entered yet another rehab facility and asked Eric to make sure his father's things were gone before she got out.

If only he could talk to Ann… He closed his eyes as a fresh wave of pain hit him.

The door flung open so hard it hit the wall, and Eric turned. Nick and Chad filled the doorway. Chad jerked his thumb over his shoulder. "What are you doing here? I thought you were going on the cruise."

Eric dropped the tape. "My luggage is in the car. I was trying to take care of a few things here first."

"You mean stalling?" Chad asked.

Raking a hand through his hair, Eric said, "Maybe. I have the feeling Ann won't be there and that will make everything so final. I am going, though. If she doesn't show, getting out of town for a change of scenery will do me some good."

"We'll give you a ride to the airport," Nick said.

"Did Noah tell you to check on me and make sure I went?" When his friends looked sheepish, Eric shook his head. "Tell him I appreciate it, but me showing up won't mean anything. Ann isn't going let me in again."

"Does this mean you're giving up?" Chad frowned.

"On Ann? Never." Eric labeled a box and set it aside. "If you want the truth, I'm afraid that she's given up on me. Her silence has been pretty loud."

"I told you before, the Snyder women are worth the fight, even when it seems all is lost," Nick said.

"Well, it definitely seems that all is lost right now, but I'm ready. Let me close up." Eric locked the estate and sent his sister a text telling her she needed to finish packing up their father's things.

• • •

Eric paced the boarding area and glanced at his watch for the hundredth time. Everywhere he turned in the chaos of people, he could see couples excited about their adventure. He'd told Ann he'd drop anything to get to her if she needed him. Could he handle a future of being just friends? He glanced at his watch again. Still no sign of her.

He'd gone through the security line and checked in. The only thing left to do was to board the ship.

"Eric?"

The familiar voice stopped him in his tracks. He turned around and saw Ann standing a few feet from him, a question in her eyes.

He swallowed. "I hope this means that you think we have a future together."

"It does." Her smile was shy, her expression one of fragile hope.

He smiled back, then it fell. "My family's lives are in shambles. I'm paying for my mom's treatment at a facility. My parents are getting divorced. Our family estate is going on the auction block. I'll always feel responsible for my mom and try to help her, so I'll never be a wealthy man. I can offer you a comfortable life, and I'll do my damnedest to make sure you never go without anything you want."

"Are you offering me yourself?"

He held his arms out. "I have nothing else. That's all that I can offer you."

"Then I accept your proposition, counselor."

He took a step forward, his heart beating fast and painfully. "You don't know the terms."

"I'm sure we can negotiate."

"Yeah?" He stopped in front of her, aching to touch her.

She put her hands on his face. "I thought about it. While it wasn't the best thing to do, I realized that you didn't lie to me about the check to hurt me."

"No, I didn't."

"I love you."

He closed his eyes as relief coursed through him. When he opened them, he touched the side of her face and leaned his forehead against hers. "Even though I'll always be a nerd at heart?"

"*Because* you're a nerd at heart. You're sexy and kind, and you have a beautiful soul, Eric Maxwell. I want to build a life with you. A home with you."

He wrapped his arms around her. "Holding you, I *am* home. I love you, Ann."

She leaned up on her tiptoes to kiss him. "Are you ready to go on board and start the rest of our lives?"

"Right beside you every step of the way." He held his hand out for hers.

Epilogue

Spring arrived in Sweet Creek, bringing with it beautiful flowers and bright green leaves on the trees, giving Ann the perfect backdrop for her wedding. Her heart hitched as she looked around the gazebo at White Point Gardens.

"Ready?" Ann turned to face her grandfather and tears welled up in her eyes.

"None of that." He chucked her gently under the chin. "It's a perfect day."

"I know. I'm marrying the man that I love."

"I meant for me. With all you girls out of the house and not needing me to matchmake, I can finally turn it into party central."

Ann laughed. "Oh, please. Don't you go throwing out a hip while I'm on my honeymoon."

"I can't promise you that. Since I stopped seeing that widow, I'm free to play the field again."

Ann grinned. "You don't fool me. A few reruns and you're asleep in your chair by eight. Six if you and Henry go fishing early in the morning."

Abby and Amelia joined them, the latter nearly at her due date. They stood together for a second, then joined hands. Wiping her eyes, Abby said, "You're beautiful, Sis."

Amelia adjusted Ann's veil headband. "Gorgeous."

Noah sniffed and blinked. "Well, my angels, I officially retire from matchmaking."

"Oh, good," Amelia said. "Because now it's our turn."

"And you know what they say about payback, Granddaddy," Ann said.

Noah's eyebrows winged upward in alarm. "What are you three up to?"

"Nothing you wouldn't do," Abby promised. "Now, places, the music is starting."

Ann squeezed her sisters' hands, and they hurried off.

"You have to promise me you three won't butt into my life," Noah said. "I have to fight off the ladies as it is. I don't need you three starting stuff."

"Don't worry, Granddaddy. We're only looking out for you." She slid her arm into the crook of his elbow as the "Wedding March" started, smiling when Noah started bargaining with her.

Everything else faded into the background as Ann climbed the steps and took her place beside Eric. The officiant began the ceremony, and within minutes, Eric and Ann were married. He kissed her as if he never wanted to stop, and Ann was in full agreement.

But then he finally lifted his head, and she looked deep into his eyes. "I'm forever yours, Eric Maxwell."

"And I'm forever yours."

Their families cheered, and in the background, Ann heard someone uncork a bottle of champagne. Noah approached with glasses for them and passed them each one.

Eric took one for himself and held it aloft.

"To my beautiful wife," he said.

"To my handsome husband," Ann added.

"To future grandkids," Noah said, and everyone laughed.

After the festivities wound down, Ann folded her hand into Eric's, looking forward to a future filled with more love and possibilities than she'd ever imagined.

Acknowledgments

I want to thank the bloggers and the readers who have supported the Stealing the Heart series. You are lovely, awesome people.

My agent, Nicole Resciniti, who was the force behind the first book in the series, thank you for your support and for saying, "We never give up." You are amazing.

For Cheryl Medina. You know why.

About the Author

Sonya Weiss is a freelance writer and author. She's addicted to great books, good movies, and Italian chocolates. She's passionate about causes that support abused animals and children. Her parents always supported her bringing stray animals home although the Great Dane rescue was a surprise.

Discover the* Stealing the Heart *series...

Stealing the Groom

There's no way Amelia Snyder is going to let her best bud Chad marry Mean Girl #1. But Amelia's at-the-altar groomnapping scheme takes a surprising turn when she ends up as the blushing bride instead. Chad's always been strictly anti-risk and definitely anti-love, and betting a lifetime of best friendship on the chance at forever might be the biggest gamble of all.

Resisting Her Rival

Abby Snyder finally has the opportunity to expand her diner now that the building next door is available. Unfortunately, she must compete with Nick Coleman to get it. Abby shared one night of intense passion with the playboy, and she's been trying to forget it ever since. But then Nick bets her the building that he can make her fall in love with him in thirty days. Nick's confident he'll get Abby to fall for him, so he'll win the building and the girl he can't get out of his mind. But even though Abby can't lose, resisting Nick is harder than she thought.

Also by Sonya Weiss

The Millionaire's Forever

CPSIA information can be obtained at www.ICGtesting.com
Printed in the USA
LVOW11s1246180416

484132LV00001B/18/P